Readers Lov

Rescue Me

"…A beautiful story of overcoming abuse, of two men who each want to be in a loving relationship and have to put the past in the past."

—Paranormal Romance Guild

Rescue Us

"Of the three books in the series, this is the crowning glory. It has everything required to make it a really good read."

—Love Bytes Reviews

Paint by Number

"This story, like most of Andrew's books is sweet and full of feelings… If you've never read a book from Andrew Grey and even if you have, I highly recommend this one."

—Open Skye Book Reviews

New Leaf

"If you love Andrew Grey's work, add this one to your shelves. It's worth it."

—Sparkling Book Reviews

In the Weeds

"This story really has it all. If you like a great second chance, small town romance, cute kids, a touch of mystery and lots of feels, this is for you."

—TTC Books and More

By ANDREW GREY

Published by DREAMSPINNER PRESS
www.dreamspinnerpress.com

By ANDREW GREY (cont'd)

Published by DREAMSPINNER PRESS
www.dreamspinnerpress.com

By ANDREW GREY (cont'd)

Published by DREAMSPINNER PRESS
www.dreamspinnerpress.com

ONLY THE BRIGHTEST STARS

ANDREW GREY

Published by
DREAMSPINNER PRESS

5032 Capital Circle SW, Suite 2, PMB# 279,
Tallahassee, FL 32305-7886 USA
www.dreamspinnerpress.com

Only the Brightest Stars
© 2023 Andrew Grey

Cover Art
© 2023 Cover Art by L.C. Chase
http://www.lcchase.com
Cover content is for illustrative purposes only and any person depicted
on the cover is a model.

Mass Market Paperback ISBN: 978-1-64108-448-2
Trade Paperback ISBN: 978-1-64108-447-5
Digital ISBN: 978-1-64108-446-8
Trade Paperback published May 2023
v1.0

Dedication: To Wallace S. and all my fans.
You make all the work worthwhile.

CHAPTER 1

"LOGAN!" HIS manager called, his footsteps echoing through the house the pain in the ass had convinced him to buy. "Where the fuck are you?"

Logan Steele sat up with a groan as he turned to the guy sprawled out on the sheets next to him. He tried to remember what the hell had gone on last night, but his mind was a blank. It had happened before, and it would probably happen again. His mouth tasted like death, but he managed to get out of bed and onto his feet. He had just reached the bathroom to get a drink of water when Carlton's voice drew nearer.

Logan didn't bother answering. Carlton would find him eventually. He thought about reaching for the half-full Stoli bottle beside the sink, but he got some water instead, rinsed his mouth, took a few painkillers, and brushed his teeth before starting the water for a shower. With any luck, that would make him feel less like he'd been run over by a truck.

He stepped around the tiled wall and into the huge shower before switching the flow to the myriad of jets in the walls and from overhead, pelting himself with hot water. He blocked out everything but the water, wishing it would wash away the dirt that he felt clinging to his very soul. Wait, that wasn't possible, because he had sacrificed that on the altar of Hollywood career success years ago. There was nothing left on the inside, and no one seemed to give a damn.

Not that they were supposed to. Logan had found out pretty quickly that he could pay people to do just about anything he wanted. He had an assistant who answered his mail and ran his social media. There were people to handle publicity, and he had Carlton to manage his life and schedule his days, making sure he showed up where he was supposed to be on time. He had a person who managed his money and paid his bills. Basically, he didn't have to do anything he didn't want to.

But none of them gave a damn about him, a kid from a dinky farming town in western Michigan who had just happened to be in the right place at the right time.

The water switched off. Logan turned and blinked at Carlton.

"You have to be at the television studio in less than an hour." Carlton tossed him a towel and turned away. "I already sent last night's diversion on his way." He shook his head as he stared at his phone.

"Who the fuck is it today?" Logan asked. His head still ached. He wished he could crawl back into bed and sleep for another few hours.

Carlton ignored him. It wasn't like he hadn't heard Logan say worse things. "Monica West. Remember her?" He lifted his gaze. Logan groaned and reached for the vodka bottle, but Carlton got to it first. "I see you do." He held the bottle. "I promised her there would be no repeat of the shit show that was your last appearance, and I mean to keep my promise. No drinking, and for God's sake, do you think you could make it through a single day without looking like a train wreck?" He left the room, and Logan ground his teeth together, his anger at himself rising.

"Do you think you could not be a giant pain in my ass?" He probably would have fired the guy a dozen times already, except Carlton was the closest thing to a friend that Logan had—which he knew was just as pathetic as the fact that he wanted a drink so fucking bad right now, he could taste it. But he knew he had to be sober and on his best behavior to promote *Knockout*, the movie he had releasing in less than a week. Somehow he had to find the energy to be charming and witty while he talked about a movie he barely remembered making.

Carlton laughed as Logan wrapped the towel around his waist and returned to the bedroom, where his clothes had been laid out on the bed. Without thinking, Logan dropped the towel and began dressing. "Drink this. It will help you feel better."

Logan sniffed and downed the glass of purple liquid. "What the hell was that?"

"A protein shake. It will give you something to counteract the booze and whatever else you've got in your stomach." He shook his head while Logan shrugged on his shirt and tucked it in, then pulled on socks and boots. Logan checked himself in the mirror and thought he didn't look half bad. Carlton shook his head. "I've set up an appointment with your personal trainer, Erik, for every day this week. You've been putting on weight, and we need to get it off and have you in shirtless shape for when you start shooting again in two weeks. You might want to spend some time in the pool to burn off a little around the middle." He patted Logan's belly as though he had a gut.

"There's nothing the fuck there," Logan snapped. "I look fine."

Carlton stepped in front of the mirror. "You do not. You have bags under your eyes, and your skin...." He shook his head. "I'll get your facialist and have Erik get you in the sauna and steam room to sweat out all the crap. Maybe that will help. Tomorrow you don't have anything until the afternoon, so you can sleep in, and then we'll get you whipped back into shape." Carlton sighed. "I'll make sure you have a pill you can take when you go to bed to help you get some rest and be ready for a full day. You're well over thirty, and I don't care if you're a man or a woman, young and pretty is what this town goes for." He looked Logan over and then pulled open one of the dresser drawers, grabbed a bottle, and dabbed a little makeup under Logan's eyes before smoothing it in. "That's better." He stepped back and nodded to himself, then checked the time and got out of the way as Logan strode out of the bedroom and down the plushly carpeted hallway to the stairs. He descended quickly and didn't pause in the hall before pulling open the front doors and heading down the walk, right into the waiting black stretch limousine.

He sank into the back seat, and Carlton got in as well. The driver closed the door, and a few seconds later they were on their way. The two of them were in their own private area. A partition separated them from the driver. Carlton pressed a button and gave instructions that Logan paid no attention to. He watched out the windows as Bel Air mansions slid past outside. Logan released a deep breath, trying to remember back to before his life had spun so profoundly out of control.

"We're running slightly late, but with a little luck with traffic, we'll get there in plenty of time and you can have a few minutes to yourself. Do you remember what you're going to talk about?" Carlton asked. "The movie, your costars, and how great it was to work with them?"

"The usual load of shit," Logan retorted.

"No. That would be when they say good things about *you*. *That's* the pile of crap," Carlton told him flatly. "They were good people and did their best. You were the one who threatened to use your costar as a stunt double and set them on fire. So you say nice things about them because you owe them for keeping their mouths shut."

Carlton went back to his phone, and Logan once again turned to the window as they glided upward and onto the freeway. Logan continued watching the scenery pass as they made their way into traffic.

"Do you ever wonder what life would be like if you hadn't gone into this business?" Logan asked. He wasn't sure if Carlton was listening.

"What life? You were on some farm in Loganville, population just above the *Walking Dead*. There was nothing there for you or anyone else." Carlton lowered his phone. "I went back there with you last year after your mother died. I saw the place, remember? There was very little there." And what little Logan might have had there was gone now. His mother had been his biggest fan and the one person he knew was always in his corner. Now there was no one left. Sure, the town had made a huge deal about him returning and had welcomed him like he was the greatest thing ever, but it felt hollow. They wanted Logan Steele, but no one remembered Wally Padgett—or cared to, for that matter. Wally had lasted a year after he'd left school and made his way to Hollywood. He'd lived on his last few pennies and gone to every audition he could find, and he'd gotten lucky. A bit part on a drama series had turned into a huge deal and gotten him his first movie, which struck low-budget gold. Everything rocketed upward from there—agents, publicity, red carpets, talk shows, the big screen, people screaming and stopping him in the damned bathroom asking for an autograph. His life had been turned on its ear overnight, and he'd been on top of the world.

Until everything changed… or maybe he was the one who changed. Logan wasn't sure. Maybe he'd never been anything at all and what he'd thought was success had been an illusion. Hollywood was so filled with magic and sets that weren't real, it was hard to know what was.

"Now there isn't anything for me anyway," Logan said softly. He tried to think of the people he'd known then, but Logan had been a theater kid in a high school without a drama department. A gay kid who didn't fit in no matter where he turned.

Carlton set aside his phone. "What's gotten into you?" he demanded. "You have a life all of those people can only dream of. One almost anyone would give their teeth for." He sat back and looked at Logan with eyes that Logan sometimes swore saw everything, and yet other times Carlton was completely blind to the truly important things.

Logan opened the refrigerator and pulled out a bottle of Evian. He eyed the bottle of vodka, wishing he could drown himself in the release it offered from all this turmoil in his head. Nothing seemed to help. The best he could do was drown his disappointment in alcohol or sex—both if he could get them. "I'm fine, just thinking about shit is all." He took a drink of the water and then set the bottle in one of the cup holders.

Carlton frowned and reached into the bottom of his case. "Do you want something to calm you down?"

Yes, yes, yes. Sometimes Logan thought he just couldn't do this anymore. He held out his hand, and Carlton placed two pills in it. Logan stared at the valium and held them for a few seconds, looking at them like they were his nemesis, but he knew that wasn't the case. What was wrong? What he was fighting was inside him. Still, if they helped him get through this damned thing….

The limousine pulled to a stop, harder than normal, and the pills went flying. They sailed through the air and landed on the floor. "I'm sorry," the driver said through the intercom.

"What the hell happened?" Carlton demanded.

"Take it easy," Logan said, suddenly able to breathe. It was almost like he had taken the damned pills. "We're fine."

"An accident happened just in front of us. I was able to avoid it," the driver reported, and then they slowly made their way forward. The accident looked bad, with three cars, one accordioned badly in the middle. A man stood outside one of the cars, blood running down the side of his face.

"Tell the driver to stop," Logan said. "Now!" The back seat seemed way too fucking small, and he needed fresh air right the fuck now. The calm from a minute earlier shattered like glass, and the shards were all coming at him like missiles. He was suddenly sixteen again and in the thick of the car accident that had taken away his father.

"Why? The police will handle it, and we have to be at the television studio in half an hour," Carlton said. "Driver, please continue."

"Stop now!" Logan said earnestly. He made sure the driver heard, and they pulled off to the side. Logan opened the door and stepped outside into a cacophony of noise and confusion. People were yelling and crying. His hands shook, and he looked up and down the street as people slowly got out of the smashed-up cars. What shocked him was how no one had bothered to stop to help. Cars slowly continued on without anyone paying attention.

"Mr. Steele," the driver said softly as he came to stand next to him. "You should get back in the car. I've called the police and they are on their way."

A man ran up to him, his brown eyes huge as saucers, jet-black hair so dark it had hints of blue. He was on the edge of panic. "Please help. My mother is in there and I can't get her out." The pleading in his eyes touched Logan deeply. The man's hand shook, and something inside Logan snapped.

"Show me," he said without thinking and grabbed the driver. "You can help too."

Logan reached the passenger side of the middle car and looked inside. A woman of about sixty sat behind the wheel, deflated air bags around her.

"Are you all right, ma'am? Can you breathe?" She sighed and nodded. It looked like the entire front of the car had shortened, pinning her in place. "Are you able to move at all? Are you hurt?"

"My head?" she said and turned to look at him. She gasped. "You're… you're…."

Logan knew that moment of recognition and near-ly backed away, but he also knew what was at stake. He had watched his father slip away from him while they waited for the emergency crew.

"I'm just trying to help." Logan reached around the steering wheel, found the lever, and pushed it up. The steering wheel moved forward a few inches, and then he pressed it up as far as it would go. "Can you move now?" he asked. "Unbuckle the seat belt…. That's it. Now, are you hurt? Can you move?" She slowly slid toward him, and he half lifted her out of the car and into his arms before carrying her away from the car. "Are you able to stand?"

She looked up at him with the same eyes as the young man. "Yes, I'm okay. But just think about it— I'm being held by Logan Steele." Her eyes got a little dreamy, and she flashed a bright smile. She rested her head against his chest, and he gently set her on her feet. She stood and got her balance. "Thank you," she said, patting his cheek.

"Mom," the young man said, hugging her fiercely. "You're okay?"

"You should all move away. I smell gasoline," Lo-gan's driver said just as the car Logan had pulled the woman out of burst into flames.

"We need to leave now or we never will," Carlton said, already tugging Logan back toward the limousine. The driver hurried around as the crowd moved away from the fire. Carlton practically pushed Logan into the limo before he climbed in himself and told the driver to get them out of there.

The limousine began to move away from the scene. It wasn't until they were moving that Logan began to shake as the adrenaline drained out of him. What the hell had he been thinking? He wasn't the fucking hero of one of those damned movies he did. Not in real life, and that fucking car had caught fire for real. This hadn't been a movie set.

"What the hell were you thinking?" Carlton asked. "You could have been hurt, and then what the fuck would have happened? You have to start shooting in two weeks, and if you'd been in that car when it caught fire…." He left the rest of his thought hanging ominously in the air.

Logan did his best to tune him out. They were minutes from the studio, and he needed to get himself into the right frame of mind—and Carlton wasn't helping.

"Just shut up," Logan snapped and reached for one of the bottles clinking in the bar. He held the fucking thing like the damned vodka bottle was going to give him the escape and comfort he needed. He was going to go on a live show that would be seen by millions of people, and he needed to be able to prepare himself, but he couldn't center his mind. He kept seeing his father slipping away next to him, and it felt like he was doing the same thing all over again. In his mind, the line between the here and now blurred with the past. He needed to try to sort it out, and that had to happen in the next few minutes.

"We're almost there, and you have to be ready…," Carlton was saying.

Logan turned away, trying to get some control once again and feeling it slipping away. He held up his hand, and finally Carlton stopped. Now only the sound of the tires on the road intruded on the space. He closed his eyes, fighting for control of the turmoil at the worst time possible.

As the car pulled to a stop, he looked out the window. Then the door opened, and Logan got out and strode up to the door being held by a man with a clipboard. He didn't pause and continued inside, past a number of people who stood out of the way. He did his best to paste on a smile, all the while his head screaming for a drink, anything to take the edge off.

"This way, Mr. Steele," a stunning Black woman in a red dress said. She gave him a smile, and her bright eyes and posture told him she'd brook no nonsense. She motioned to a dressing room, and he went inside and sat in one of the chairs in front of a set of mirrors. "You'll go on as the final guest of the show. We want to be able to build up to your appearance." Again, her voice was solid, and he needed that. "You're going to do a great job."

He turned in the chair. "You know, I really hate doing these things." He was an actor, and he should be able to get in front of people and just do his thing. He had done it all his adult life. This was just another scene he had to play.

"Yes. I've heard that." She stepped closer, her heels clicking on the tile floor. "But just talk to Monica. Don't even think about anything or anyone else. She wants her show to go well. We have a great teaser clip from the film, and she's going to ask you the basic questions." For some reason her voice soothed him, and he cracked his eyes open and actually smiled. "Can I bring you anything?"

Logan swallowed hard. "I'd kill for a triple vodka right now, but maybe a diet soda with ice." He gripped the chair arms to keep his hands from shaking. Early on in his career he had done things like this all the time and had never given them a second thought. Maybe then he'd had nothing to lose so he'd gone for it. But now he had a ton of people depending on him to deliver, and he felt every ounce of that weight. Or maybe that was all a crock of shit and he truly was washed up and the last one to realize it.

"Thank you," Logan said and held out his hand. She shook it and then stepped away as Carlton charged into the room like the proverbial bull in the china shop. He was followed by the makeup artist, who placed a paper around Logan's collar to protect his clothes and silently went to work getting him ready, with Carlton issuing instructions. Now all Logan had to do was sit and pray that this segment was good and that he could pull himself together for long enough to make a good impression—to make the audience happy enough to want to see a film that he'd been too out of it to remember.

HE'D DONE it. That was all he could think about once he was back in the limousine. The weight was lifted. Logan could hear the audience roaring their excitement when he'd come on stage, and that had energized him. He told a few stories he'd remembered about shooting and enthused about his costars, putting them in the best light. In the back of his mind, something had switched on as soon as he sat down, and he had all this energy. He and Monica had laughed and acted like they had little inside jokes, and Logan had smiled and even brought the other guests into the conversation. In short, he'd killed it.

"That was okay, but you seemed a little hyped up," Carlton said. "I doubt anyone else noticed it. Monica sure seemed to be having a good time." In three seconds, Logan's good mood slipped away, flowing out of the car and drifting away on the wind passing outside. Carlton patted his knee twice. "It was a good spot, and online it's getting good comments."

"Then we're done for the day?" Logan asked. What he needed was a day of peace and quiet.

"Yes. Your trainer will be at the house at three this afternoon. Other than that, there's nothing for the rest of the day." Carlton settled back in the seat, and Logan stayed quiet. Maybe that wasn't such a bad idea. Logan pulled out his phone, checked the time, and answered a few messages from his agent as well as one from his business manager.

"I want something to eat," Logan said. "Maybe we could stop...." God, he wanted a burger so bad. Maybe something familiar would soothe his jangled nerves. What he wouldn't give for a Big Mac and fries right about now.

"Already set. I have lunch waiting at the house when you get back so you can be ready to go with your trainer." Fucking hell, he couldn't even eat what he wanted to. "You have to get in shape, and that's going to take some effort. You asked me to make sure you were ready for this part, and I promised to do my best."

Logan knew that was true, but what he really wanted was some real food and a chance to be around a few real people, talking about real things and not this eternal Hollywood bubble that warped everything until it was unrecognizable. Rather than fight Carlton, who was only doing what Logan had asked, he once again looked out the window, right leg bouncing slightly as they rode.

After they arrived at the house, Logan had lunch, watched the entertainment news, and finally poured himself a drink. He savored the cool, clear liquid. Ice clinked in the glass, and he tried to relax. It didn't take long for the drink to turn into a second one, and then Logan put the bottle away. The jitters had subsided, and he didn't feel like he was going to climb out of his skin. Switching to water, he changed clothes and was ready when Jason arrived for his training session.

"You're doing well," Jason encouraged as he put Logan through his paces. "We want to work you good, but not push it too much."

Still, Logan worked hard. That had never been his issue. Hard work was something he'd been brought up with, and once he started the workout, he threw himself into it. Sweat rolled down his back and chest as he went through Jason's nearly sadistic routine. Once that was done, he spent half an hour on the treadmill, watching television to take his mind off the time. Then he showered and changed, figuring he'd relax out by the pool and give himself some down time.

The water shimmered in the southern California sunshine, and he sat back on the lounge under the pergola with a bottle of water, his mind clear and finally quiet.

"I thought you could use one of these." A martini slid into his field of vision.

He set the glass aside. "What are you doing here?" Logan asked Grant, a neighbor and friend of sorts, who stood next to the chair in one of the smallest bathing suits known to man. They had had a thing—very short-lived—maybe a year and a half ago. Nothing had come of it, but that never stopped Grant from hanging around.

He plopped himself down on the other chair, making sure his ample assets were on display. "I heard that a certain movie star was all alone and might need some company." Which was code for he'd seen the car pull in and figured Logan was home so he popped over. "I asked a few friends over this afternoon, but since you're alone…." He leaned back.

"Grant, I need a day of quiet."

The gate swung open, and a group of guys strode into the yard before he could finish his thought. He should have known. This was Grant, a force of nature, the ultimate party boy, and he definitely knew how to get things started.

"Don't worry. I figured you wouldn't want to come over, so we brought the party to you." Grant grinned as the guys all approached carrying something in their hands. Food, bottles—everything for a party came through the gate, along with a parade of some of the hottest men ever, who slipped off their shirts and shorts before wandering around the pool. Music started, and Grant directed everything with ease, though he hardly moved from his spot.

"Do I ever let you down?" Grant flashed Logan his biggest smile, and Logan sighed. What the hell, it was a party. He took the icy glass that Grant offered and downed half of it in a few gulps. The warmth spread through him. Then he finished the drink and reached for another.

CHAPTER 2

"ARE YOU sure you're okay?" Brit Stimple asked quietly, standing off to the side and out of the area being used for shooting. He didn't want to talk very long because his mother thought he was waiting tables rather than as crew for adult films. Hopefully they were done for the day and he could go on to his real job—or at least what he thought of as his real job. This one paid the bills, but it was also his big secret and one he had no intention of adding to his résumé.

"I'm fine, honey, so stop worrying. I already called the insurance company, and they're taking care of everything." At least she sounded all right, and that alone calmed Brit down after the terrible morning they'd had. A man hadn't been paying attention and had rear-ended their car hard on Beverly Drive, and that had pushed them into the car in front. Brit had been able to get out, but his mom had needed some help. And man, had it shown up—in the form of Logan Steele. He'd gotten Brit's mom out of the car, and Brit vowed to see every one of his movies at least twice just to say thank you. "It's all under control, and I got to cop a feel of Logan Steele." She giggled, and Brit knew she was back to her old self. "I'll talk to you later. I have news to spread." She hung up, and Brit put his phone back in his pocket and turned toward the director as he quickly reviewed what they'd shot. He declared they were done for the day, and Brit grabbed his jacket and snagged a few power bars off what passed for the catering table, ready to get out of there.

Brit scooted out of the building and to his car, then hurried away from the San Fernando Valley as quickly as he could. He always felt dirty whenever he was done, but it paid the bills and allowed him to keep his tiny apartment in West Hollywood, which was where he was heading. Brit had managed to get a part in the West Hollywood Players all-male version of *Oklahoma!*—or *Oklahomo!*, as he referred to it in his mind. His phone rang through the car while he was on the freeway, and Brit answered it.

"Hey, Clive, what's going on?" he asked.

"Oh, honey. I just heard. Are you okay?" Clive gushed a million miles an hour. He and Clive had been neighbors and best friends since they were five. They'd each lost their father, Brit's to cancer and Clive's to a divorce and remarriage to a girl three years older than Clive.

"I'm fine," he breathed. "I'm on my way to the theater now. Things ran over, and I'm trying to get there.

Don't let any of those queens snap a garter because I'm not there yet." Acting and theater were the things he loved, and he wouldn't miss a performance if his life depended on it.

"Okay. I'll tell them," he agreed. "Are you sure you're okay?"

Brit rolled his eyes and slowed as he came upon heavy traffic. "What do you think? I spent the morning dealing with an accident, but managed to get to the day job on time, and there I spent the day watching eight guys suck and fuck in every position known to man while Harvey, the director from hell, enlisted me to be the voice of one of the guys because I can apparently fake complete and total ecstasy better than anyone on the damned planet." Brit was wrung out.

Clive snickered and then lost it on the other side of the phone. "I'm sorry, honey, but that's what you get when you're the king of porn voice-overs." He continued laughing.

"It's not funny." Traffic started forward. "Do you know how frustrating that is? I'm there just off camera. 'Oh baby, that's it. Yeah… fuck me harder… oh yeah… fuuuuccckkk… oh yeah, oh yeah… fuuuuccckkkk….' And I don't even get to do the fucking. Not that I'm ever letting anyone film me having sex, because I don't want to break the cameras." He was well aware that he didn't have the body or the internal fortitude it took to act like getting rammed up the ass by the biggest dick on the planet was an experience that completely rocked his world… on camera. "But still, hours of it, and one of the guys is great. You'd swear he was over the moon—until he opens his mouth and blows the illusion, if you'll pardon the pun, completely to hell."

"And that's where you come in... sort of," Clive chimed in. "Do you at least get paid for the voice-overs in addition to what else you do?" He was having way too much fun with this.

"Yeah, I do. But I keep hoping something will happen and I won't need to do the porn thing anymore." Though he liked eating, and this paid the bills and allowed him to do what he really loved—theater. Still, he shrugged and breathed a sigh of relief as he merged over to take his exit. "Anyway, I'm getting off the freeway. I'll be at the theater in, like, ten minutes."

"I saved you a place to park," Clive said, still chuckling as he hung up.

Brit knew that sometimes life was stranger than fiction; he only wished that someone else's life would take center stage in that category for a few minutes. He wasn't a complicated person. Brit's greatest wish was to be able to make a living doing what he loved— preferably in front of the camera and with his clothes on. A chuckle rose up as the thought flashed through his mind. That was something he didn't have the balls for, and he laughed at his own internal pun. He liked to think he had a gift, but then so did every other actor in Hollywood. No, Brit had seen tons of movies where the part of a lifetime came with strings that cost someone more than they were willing to pay. Brit hoped to hell that if he got the chance, he'd be strong enough to resist temptation and stay true to himself. But then again, he would only ever know if opportunity actually came knocking, and so far it hadn't.

AN ALL-MALE version of *Oklahoma!* He supposed there were worse ways to kill a little time until the clubs really got going, and the theater had a bar. Logan sat, and one of the servers took his martini order. Of course he'd be recognized, but the staff must have been trained well enough that no one bothered him or asked for an autograph.

"Are you sure about this?" he asked Grant, who sat next to him. He'd brought a couple of the boys along too, but they seemed deep in their own conversation.

Grant shrugged and hefted his glass. "What does it matter? If it's bad, we'll drink a little and then head out. It's not like we have to actually stay." He downed his cocktail and ordered another as the curtain went up.

The costuming—what there was of it—was basic and a little cartoonish, which made it charming. Logan raised his drink to finish it and got ready to go as Curly came on. Most of the cast had a community theater vibe about them, but not this guy. He had intensity and a flow to his movements. It took Logan just a few seconds to recognize the guy from the car accident. He set his drink on the table, smiling at Curly's antics, unable to take his eyes off him.

"I think we can go," Grant said, but Logan waved him away, not saying a word or taking his gaze from the stage. "Logan...."

He waved his hand again without turning, and Grant grew quiet. Not that Logan would have noticed or cared. He smiled and laughed with the man's comic timing. The other actors didn't take themselves too seriously and had fun with the story, which made it all the more enjoyable.

The first half ended, and Logan realized his drink sat untouched and that he was smiling. He pushed the glass away, ready for more of the show.

"I think we've seen enough," Grant said.

"Then leave," Logan said more sharply than he intended. But on second thought, he didn't really care. He'd spent over an hour without worrying about movies or box office receipts or anything else, and he wanted to hold on to that if he could.

Grant left the table, and Logan just sat still. When Grant returned with more drinks, he set one in front of Logan, who sipped it absently until the curtain went up again. He promptly forgot about it as soon as Curly returned to the stage.

THE PLAY was a hit, at least as far as the audience was concerned. The house was packed, and the applause went on and on. Brit was sweaty and sticking to the cow-patterned chaps he wore in his part as Curly. The company had camped it up big-time, and the laughter told them all that it was working. The play wasn't art and never would be, but the audience had a good time, and the actors always made a point of responding to their reactions in order to bring everyone into the experience.

"Guys," Clive breathed as though he were about to either pass out or plotz at any second. "You'll never guess who's out front." He practically bounced from foot to foot. "Logan Steele and a bunch of his friends. Jan in the box office said they just showed up, and she made special room for them." He rubbed his hands together.

"He must be here to see me," Joshua said. He'd played Lawrence, Curly's love interest.

Clive flounced over. "Sorry, Miss Thang, but everything is not about you." He bumped Brit's hip. "He asked to talk to Curly."

Joshua rolled his eyes. "My ass."

"And maybe he'd be asking for you if you had one," Clive retorted, and a chorus of *oooooh*s went through the entire cast as Clive pressed Brit to his seat. "Now you, honey, get that costume off and into some cute clothes." He rummaged through a suitcase and came up with black jeans and a light blue T-shirt. "Grease yourself into these if you have to and get out there pronto. I don't know how long he's going to stay." Clive practically tugged off his costume, and Brit changed as quickly as he could, sucking in his breath and everything else to get those pants on.

"There's no way I'm getting into this shirt." His arms were stuck over his head, but Clive pulled it down. "It's too small. Everything is."

"Honey, this shows off all your assets, so you just go with it. Now put some shoes on and get out there before he leaves." Clive waited three seconds—just long enough for Brit to get his shoes on—and then he was pressing him out of the room and down the hall to the side door.

Brit pushed it open and stumbled right into Logan Steele's arms—*strong* arms. Brit's breath hitched as he was surrounded by the manliest scent he had ever inhaled. He lifted his gaze and stared into the same blue eyes he had seen on the screen in the theater—except these were filled with loneliness and yearning that hit Brit in the gut. *That* was something he hadn't seen at the movies.

"Umm, thanks," Brit said as he got his feet under him. "I'm okay." He turned to glare at Clive just before the door closed behind him. Brit pushed past the flutters and stood taller. "I wanted to thank you for helping my mom and me this afternoon. I really appreciate it."

He seemed a little taken aback for a second, before composing himself. "How is she?" Logan asked, his gaze burning into Brit like a blazing fire, radiating heat that started at the base of his spine and went up and down his entire body in seconds. "I'm sorry we had to leave in such a hurry. Did everything work out?"

"Yes. Everything is fine," Brit answered, his throat dry.

"Logan, are you going to introduce us to your little friend?" a man asked from one of the front tables near the stage.

Brit bristled and was about to cut the guy to shreds, but Logan beat him to it.

"No, I don't think so, Grant," he snapped and then turned back to Brit with a smile that would melt butter. "Do you have to stay here? Can you leave?"

Brit nodded and was swept away. "What about your friends? And you don't even know my name." He was a little confused and overwhelmed.

"They are perfectly capable of getting a ride home, and they're not my friends. They're more hangers-on." He continued heading for the door, holding Brit's hand. "And I know your name. Your friend told me what it was. Is Brit short for something?"

Brit found himself being dragged along in Logan's wake, like iron flakes to a magnet.

"Brighton Stevens," he answered. "But everyone called me Brit, and it just stuck."

"Logan," Grant called as he strode up, "what's going on? We're planning to head on over to a club a few blocks away. You should come with us and bring your new friend."

Brit narrowed his gaze. "What's with you?" he asked, moving away from Logan. "I'm right here, and

I have a name, and I'll decide where I go and what I do." He looked the guy over. "No one's telling me that. Certainly not some eunuched Ken doll wannabe, all primped and pressed, but with nothing to offer where it counts." He turned away and headed for the door, not looking back to see if Logan or anyone else followed him. He figured he'd get in his car and drive home.

"Brit," Logan said as he approached from behind him.

Brit stopped again. "Why don't you just go with your friends?" It had been a long day, and he was tired and had put up with all he could.

"I'd rather go with you," Logan said in his aged-whiskey-rough voice.

Brit still resisted. Things like this didn't happen to him. Movie stars didn't just walk into his theater and take him by the hand.

"I need to tell my friends," Brit told him. Maybe he was a fool for even thinking of going with Logan at all.

Clive hurried out from the back, with half the rest of the cast following behind him. "We'll get your car to your place for you." Clive hugged Brit. "Go and have a good time. It isn't every day that a movie star takes a shine to you." He patted Brit on the back and then herded the other guys away. "Call me tomorrow!" he threw back over his shoulder with a smile.

"Shall we go?" Logan asked, practically sweeping Brit off his metaphorical feet and out of the theater to where the same limousine he'd seen at the accident waited. The driver got out, but Logan waved him away and opened the door himself. Brit slid into another world, and then Logan climbed in and closed the door, and the car glided away, almost like it wasn't moving at all.

"This is something else," Brit commented, trying not to sound like some hick, even though he was surrounded by automotive luxury he'd never even dreamed about.

"Would you like a drink?" Logan pulled out a bottle from the rack and poured himself a glass. Brit shook his head and then changed his mind and took a water. He didn't want to drink anything else. This would be over as soon as the sun came up, and he wanted to remember every second. "Do you want to go somewhere?"

"I am hungry. I don't usually eat before shows…," Brit started, and Logan pressed a button.

"Please call in an order somewhere—steak, salad, the works. And have it delivered to the house. Thank you." Logan let up on the button, and they continued their ride.

"Why are you doing this?"

"I didn't expect to see you again after this morning," Logan answered as he stretched out his long legs. "Then one of the guys suggested we go out, and he had tickets to the show, so we went. He figured it would be a hoot, but then I saw you."

"I heard the guys talking and being snarky."

Logan nodded. "But I shut them up because you were good, and I couldn't take my eyes off you in those silly cow-print chaps." He finished his drink and poured himself another. Brit reached for the bottle, and when Logan handed it to him, he recapped it and put it back in the bar. Logan stared for a second and then continued, "You had real presence. Just like this morning. My manager had to drag me away."

"I can't believe it was you who came to the rescue." Brit was going to have a hard time forgetting that. It had been worthy of a movie scene. "Mom is fine and just as feisty as ever, thanks to you. But I'm wondering why you're doing this with me." He took a sip of water. "I'm just some guy in the play you saw tonight. You helped me, and I'm grateful, but that isn't a reason to take me on the great limo ride back to your house." He was really trying to figure this out. "What is it you want?"

Logan set his glass in one of the holders. "I don't know. Maybe some time with someone who isn't part of the business." He leaned forward, those intense eyes meeting Brit's. "Why did you come with me? Was it because you wanted something from me?"

Brit shrugged. "No."

"Why not? Everyone wants something—the studio, managers. Hell, my gardener once asked me if I'd look at his script. In this town, every single person is looking for something or wants something. A leg up, a word, something."

Brit shook his head. "That must be one fucking lonely life." He drank some more water, still unable to believe he was in a limousine with Logan Steele and trying to figure out what about him had caught his attention. "Yeah, I want a career and to stop having to do production and voice-over work for adult films. And I'd like to be able to get parts where my wardrobe wasn't sewn, duct-taped, and pinned together from fabric bought down at the mall because it was on sale. But not at any cost, and I'm not going to sell myself or my soul to get it." He sat back in the seat, figuring he might as well enjoy the ride. "And I'm not going to... I don't know... parlay a limousine ride into a career move." He knew he had talent, but so did most of the other people scraping to try to get noticed in this business.

Logan turned to look at him, staring into Brit's eyes as he reached for the bottle again. Brit placed his hand on Logan's, and he set his empty glass aside. "I don't understand you," Logan admitted.

"What's not to understand?" Brit asked. "I'm a guy who works hard for what I have, and I don't think that someone is going to just come along and give me what I want on a silver platter. And I don't want anything from you." He smiled and slid closer to Logan. "Besides, I wasn't the one who came up to you, remember? I seem to recall that you were the one who latched on to me and asked me if I wanted to go." He held Logan's gaze, those huge, incredible eyes staring back into his. "I think I should be the one to ask you what it is you want. I have nothing to give a guy like you."

Logan lifted his hands and slid them along Brit's cheek, then tugged him down and into a kiss that sent electricity coursing through him. Ten minutes ago, Brit had been tired and hungry; now, in seconds, he was energized and on fire. Logan tasted of alcohol sharpness, which quickly faded to the deep, rich, mellow taste of the man underneath. Brit returned the kiss, passion hitting him like a freight train. He had been with guys before—more than he wanted to admit to—but none of them had set him on fire with just a kiss.

He was tempted to press Logan back on the seat and take everything he could possibly get, but instead he pulled back as the limousine made a turn and slowed. Brit blinked as the world around him righted itself and returned to focus, centering on Logan, who still had his hand on Brit's cheek. "You're something else," Logan whispered.

Brit shrugged. "I'm just me." He started when the door opened, not even realizing they had stopped. Man, how had he missed that, and what the hell had happened to him? For a few seconds it felt like he had been pulled into another dimension containing only him and Logan.

Logan didn't move, and the door stayed open. Maybe he'd felt the same way. Brit didn't know. But then the spell broke, and Logan climbed out of the car and extended his hand. Brit took it, and Logan led him up a cobbled walk with lighted landscaping all around. It looked like a fairy-tale scene, with a riot of color everywhere. The air carried the sweet scent of the flowers, and Brit couldn't help pausing to inhale.

"Come inside," Logan whispered, guiding him through the front door and into a house that took Brit's breath away.

The entire back wall of the main floor was glass looking out over the pool, which shimmered with light. Palm trees lined the yard, carpeted with a perfect lawn and still more flowers. Logan walked over to the bar just off the kitchen. "What can I get you?"

"Nothing, thanks," Brit said, still captivated by the modern yet surprisingly warm space. He liked it.

A cork popped, and Logan handed him a glass of sparkling wine.

"We have to have something to make this special," Logan said. He took a sip from his glass as the back door opened and the driver came in and placed a bag on the counter.

"Thank you," Brit prompted, bumping Logan's shoulder.

"What?" Logan asked.

Brit shook his head. "He was nice."

"Thank you," Logan said with a smile, and the driver left.

"Do you know his name?" Brit asked as he started unpacking the food.

"I use a limousine service, so the drivers vary. But you're right. That was good of him." Logan drained his glass and poured himself some more, then got plates and silverware and took a seat at the bar, patting the chair next to him. Brit climbed up and opened the packages. His mouth watered at the perfect steak that awaited him. This was no regular takeout container, that was for sure, because there was a pack in the bottom to make sure the meat stayed hot. Logan plated the food and slid Brit's over to him.

He took a bite and rolled his eyes, it was so good. Logan chuckled next to him. "What did you do before you were a movie star?" Brit asked.

Logan took a bite of his salad. "I was a mechanic for a while. Terrible at it. I waited tables. I think I was awful at that too, because I kept getting the orders wrong. I always wanted to be an actor, but I got lucky as hell. One of my auditions got me a small part in a TV series. That episode had a guest director, and he offered me a part in his next movie. From there, everything took off." Logan slowly continued eating while Brit dug in.

"Family?" Brit asked, and Logan shook his head. "I see."

"You?" Logan asked.

"I have friends. You saw Clive tonight, and you saved my mom this morning." Brit placed his hand on Logan's shoulder. "I don't think I will ever be able to thank you enough for what you did. My mother is going to tell all her friends that she got to spend her morning in the arms of Logan Steele." He lightly stroked down Logan's rock-hard arm. "That was really brave of you."

"No." Logan drank some more and poured himself another glass. Brit got up and grabbed a bottle of water, pushed the wineglass away, and handed Logan the water instead. The stare he fixed Brit with could have frozen the water in the bottle solid, but Brit pretended not to see it. It wasn't as though he had anything against alcohol, but the way Logan seemed to suck it down was concerning. Brit had seen what alcohol could do to a person. His father had left, but before that, it had been months of his parents fighting and plenty of alcohol-fueled rages that had left Brit hiding under his bed while his father ranted at his mom. After that, he'd grown up without a dad, and as he looked back on it, he and his mom were both better off.

"Sore topic?" Brit asked. "It was just Mom and me. Dad found a younger model and left the two of us high and dry." He finished the steak. "Aren't you going to eat?"

"I'm supposed to be watching my weight for a role that starts in a few weeks."

Brit reached over and stole the potato off Logan's plate. "There. Now it's diet. So eat." He got the feeling that a lot of Logan's calories came in liquid form, which wasn't a good idea as far as he was concerned.

"What about you? Will you eat all that?" Logan asked.

Brit dug right in. He finished his steak, the vegetables, and part of his own potato. He left the one he nabbed on the plate. "I need my energy." He grinned and tapped Logan's plate, pleased when he started eating. He gave Logan a glare when he stopped, and Logan finished the steak. Brit placed the dishes in the sink and looked around again. "I love the tiger," he said, pointing to a large sculptural piece of a tiger stalking its prey.

"I do too. Art isn't something I know anything about, though. My decorator helped me pick it out." Logan took Brit's hand again, and Brit slipped off the stool. Logan slid open the glass doors, and they stepped out into the night. He led Brit to the lounge chairs beside the pool. Brit stretched out, and Logan did the same on the one beside him. "I love it out here. I just wish there were stars. It's about the only thing I miss from Michigan." Brit held Logan's hand and stayed silent. "Well, that and my parents."

Brit squeezed his hand. "I grew up here, and I know how you feel." He kept his eyes directed toward the sky, which glowed with the lights of the city, only a few stars bright enough to shine through. He concentrated on those few.

Logan sat up on his lounger, and Brit did the same, turning to face him, their knees alternating. Logan leaned forward, and Brit did too, as though he were on a string. The kiss was just as hot and intense as it had been in the car. Logan knelt down and drew Brit closer, holding him tightly, as though he expected Brit to bolt.

Brit slipped his fingers through Logan's soft hair, cradling his head, deepening the kiss to the point he could think of nothing else. He knew he was already in trouble with the intensity between them. This was overwhelming, and he needed a chance to think—but Logan only pulled back far enough for them to inhale before slamming their lips together once more, stealing Brit's breath and wiping aside his better judgment.

Logan stood and tugged Brit to his feet. Brit gripped him tighter, practically climbing Logan. He was so turned on he couldn't think straight, and when Logan moved, they went together.

"Where are we going?" Brit asked through his lust-induced haze. Logan felt so good against him, holding him with hot, solid, powerful arms, and yet there was something almost desperate in him. Brit could feel it. The thing was, it wasn't the usual kind of desperation, but something Logan was looking for so hard and yet seemed unable to find. Brit knew that feeling. It had been a constant part of his life since his father had left him behind.

"I thought we could go upstairs."

Brit backed away. "I don't think so." All his friends would think he was crazy for turning down sex with Logan Steele, but something in the back of his mind told him that was not a good idea. At least not now. He gazed into Logan's searching eyes. "Look, it's been great hanging out with you. Thank you for dinner. And if I can make my brains work after the way you kissed me into next week, I'm going to ask you if someone could drive me home. I can get an Uber otherwise. It's no big deal." Maybe he was making the biggest mistake of his life.

Logan backed away. "I see."

Brit smiled, keeping his eyes on Logan, holding him without touching. "I don't think you do. But that's okay." He closed the distance between them. "You're a great guy, and I thank you for what you did for my mom… and for giving me a night I'll remember forever." He took Logan's hand. "But I think it's best if I say good night and go on home." He squeezed Logan's fingers.

"I'll drive you home," Logan offered, but Brit shook his head. "Then just a minute." He pulled out his phone and texted, then waited a few seconds. "They'll be here in a few minutes. The driver will take you wherever you want to go." The energy inside Logan seemed to have drained away, and his eyes had lost some of the sparkle from earlier.

Brit slipped his arms around Logan's neck and pulled him down, planting one on him that left him shuddering and had Logan quivering in his arms. Then he drew back, smiling at how huge Logan's eyes had grown. His cheeks were flushed, and his lips were swollen and oh-so-kissably succulent. Damn, it was so hot that Brit was able to do that to him.

"Will I see you again?" Logan whispered.

Brit let his hands fall back to his side. "That, Logan Steele, is up to you." He stroked Logan's cheek, holding his hand there just long enough for Logan to lean into the touch, and then he slowly walked to the door, stepping outside just as the car pulled into the drive.

CHAPTER 3

CARLTON BREEZED in a little after nine the following morning while Logan was on the treadmill. He paused in the doorway to Logan's workout room. "Are you a pod person?" Carlton asked.

"What?" Logan asked as he sped up the machine. "You said I needed to get into shape, so I'm doing that. There's half a whole-wheat bagel there if you need something to eat, or you can make a protein shake." He had had what he wanted and was now in the zone. "What's going on today?"

"I promised you a day off, and that's today. Tomorrow you have the premiere, and then it will be all-out publicity until you return to the set." Carlton had his phone out. "You're booked pretty solid."

He left the room, and Logan put his ear buds in and let the music take him. He needed another fifteen minutes and then he could shower and relax until the trainer arrived.

Once he'd cooled down, Logan toweled off the sweat and hurried up to his bathroom, where he showered. Then he joined Carlton at the snack bar, where he was deep in his phone. "I see you had quite a day. The pictures of the pool party are all over Twitter and Instagram, though thankfully you aren't in any of them. Good job for that."

Logan shook his head. "What does it matter?"

Carlton set down his phone. "You have a reputation as the life of the party already. Being tagged in something or referenced in an Instagram post will pass quickly. But pictures of you tying one on aren't going to endear you to anyone, especially if your past co-stars or directors see them and decide to comment." He glared at Logan like he was a child to be scolded. "This is a bunch of wannabes saying they were here." Carlton continued scrolling. "Though this is interesting."

"What?" Logan groaned. He had been proud of himself for getting up, eating well, and working out.

"There are pictures of you outside a theater in West Hollywood and a few of you leaving with someone. The post says it was one of the actors in the show." He glared at his phone. "Who is this guy, and do we need to be worried?"

Logan sighed. "No. His name is Brit, and he's the guy whose mother I helped yesterday at the accident. I went to the theater with some of the guys, and he was in the show." Logan wasn't going to tell Carlton that he hadn't been able to take his eyes off Brit the entire show and that the guy was pretty amazing. All night and most of the morning, Logan had wondered where he was and what he was doing. Even now, as he sat on the stool Brit had used when they'd eaten last night, he held on to a bottle of water and imagined what he and Brit could be doing if he had managed to convince him to stay.

"Did you bring him back here?" Carlton asked. "You know you need to be careful. Sure, everyone knows that Logan Steele is gay, but again, no one wants to see him picking up guys. Being gay is more acceptable now, but it's the family gays that most people like." Sometimes Carton sounded so damned superior. Still, that didn't mean he was wrong.

"It was a good evening," Logan said without elaborating.

Carlton sighed dramatically. "Do you need me to go upstairs and tell him to hit the road?"

"No. Brit didn't stay." Logan went around and pulled out the blender to mix up a protein shake. He added some fresh berries to ramp up the taste. "We had dinner and then talked out by the pool…." He turned on the blender to drown out whatever snark Carlton might have delivered. "Then I called him a limo and he went home." Logan poured the shake into two glasses and offered Carlton one. He thought about adding some vodka to the shake. Carlton was really getting on his nerves, and he wanted that mellow feeling he'd had last night with Brit. Of course, Carlton would have a fit if he did that, so he downed the drink and put the glass in the sink.

Carlton slipped off his stool and leaned over the counter. "He didn't stay?" Logan shook his head. "And all you did was talk and have dinner?"

"Yes," Logan snapped.

Of course Carlton ignored it. "What did he want?"

"Actually, nothing at all. He kissed me good night and asked if he could get a ride home." Logan swallowed hard as he thought about the kisses and how he swore his heart had felt them. There was something there, and Logan didn't even have a phone number or any way to contact him other than by going back to the theater for another performance. Hell, he didn't even know his last name—though that would be easy enough to find out using the theater's website. "And just so we're clear, I asked him to stay. Hell, I wanted to. Instead, he was gentle and kind and told me no."

"Okay. That's a first," Carlton whispered. "Did he want to see you again?"

Logan didn't answer, turning to leave the room. He had work to do, and he needed Carlton to get on with his. All these questions were getting damned close to things he didn't want to discuss. He couldn't quite figure out what Brit had meant when he'd said that meeting again was up to him. Did Brit want to see him again or not?

"Logan, the guy was nice to you, didn't want anything, and then didn't sleep with you." Carlton came up behind him.

"So what? Not everyone scores every time," Logan snapped.

Carlton scoffed. "Was last night about scoring? Or was it about something else?"

"I don't fucking know. Okay? Guys are interested in me because I'm Logan Steele. We all have a good time, and in the morning, they leave, or you make sure they go. It's simple, easy, and predictable. Everyone goes on, no harm, no foul, and that's that." Hell, Logan didn't even know half their names, and he didn't really care. They were fun diversions. But last night had been so very different, and the fucking thing was he couldn't figure out why.

"Maybe predictability isn't all it's cracked up to be," Carlton told him as though he was some sort of sage.

Logan didn't have an answer, so he flipped him off and went to put on his suit to take a swim. Cryptic answers made him want a drink.

"NO THANKS, Grant," Logan said as he settled in the back of the limousine. The driver closed the door. He was dressed to blend in and had pointedly not shaved that morning so he had a little scruff. Sunglasses were out, but he wore a hat and ill-fitting clothes. That should be enough to throw people off until the lights went down. "I'm already on my way out for the evening." He reached for an aged whiskey and poured a little over ice, the cubes clinking as he spoke.

"But you're always up for a party, and this one should be really special. I hired a few of the guys from one of the studios in the valley, and damn, they're fucking hot. You just have to come. And Randy's brought some really special shit. It will blow your fucking mind."

Damn, that was tempting, but Logan was already on his way. Not that he couldn't change destinations with a request.

Logan downed the smoky liquid, the burn sliding down his throat, giving him a little courage and soothing his nerves. "I think I'll have to sit this one out for now. Though I may stop by later. Have fun." He set his phone on the seat. His leg bounced on the floor as he wondered if Brit even wanted to see him. On a whim, he'd bought tickets for Brit's show tonight. It was the only place he knew he might find him, and tomorrow was the final night of the run, so he had to either take a chance or give up.

Maybe Brit didn't want to see him and last night had been his imagination.

Logan found himself pouring another glass of whiskey just to try to take the edge off and calm his anxiety.

"Do you really think this is something I need to see?" Roger, an old friend in the business, asked from behind his phone in the seat next to him.

"I asked you to come as a favor, and it's only for a few hours," Logan told him. "What is it going to hurt? You'll laugh, see a show, and I'll have you home with your wife and kids before you turn into a pumpkin. I promise." He rolled his eyes, wishing he could shake the anxiety that gripped him.

The ride from Bel Air to the theater took twenty minutes with traffic, and he kept himself occupied with his phone for most of the trip.

"Don't pull up to the theater. Let us out a block or two away, and I'll call when we're ready to be picked up," he told the driver, and they got out when the car came to a stop. The driver pulled away, and Logan walked the block and a half to the theater, head down. He presented their tickets, and he and Roger were shown to a table in the middle of the theater. He ordered drinks from the server and held the cool glass in his hands. God, he hated being this anxious about anything.

When he'd gotten his first real break, Logan had thought he could do anything. He had charged into every performance and every situation as though he were invincible and nothing could touch him. And at that time, nothing had. His performances were top-notch, and he was on top of the world. He tried to think of when that had changed and when Logan Steele had gotten all nervous and foot-bouncy over a guy. Logan glanced around, glad to see that no one was paying attention to him. As the lights dimmed, he lifted his gaze to the stage, where Brit made his entrance in those damned cow-print chaps. Roger laughed next to him, which was encouraging.

Logan couldn't help smiling, because the costume didn't matter. After two minutes, he didn't see it any longer. Brit's light and energy shone through everything. Logan barely registered Roger sitting next to him. The audience laughed and giggled at the comic antics on stage, but Logan's gaze had locked onto Brit, and he seemed to hold his breath when Brit was gone, only releasing it once Brit reappeared in a scene.

The audience was encouraged to interact and have a ball, and the actors played along with them. Just like the night before, it pulled Logan into the experience—especially when Brit sat on the edge of the stage and talked in character to the audience as though they were all old friends… and he did it with such little effort.

Never in Logan's life had two hours flown by so quickly, but before he knew it, the audience was on their feet, applauding as the house lights came up. Roger stood next to him, grinning from ear to ear and applauding madly.

"What did you think?" Logan asked. He had purposely not told Roger specifically why they were there, other than as a chance for him to scout some new talent.

"Fucking hilarious. Who wrote the show?" he asked as he thumbed through the handprinted booklet. "Ah, a group effort, it seems." He folded the booklet and placed it in his pocket. "Was there someone you specifically wanted me to see?"

Logan sat back down while most of the rest of the audience filed out. "Yes, but—"

Roger chuckled and clapped him on the shoulder. Then he motioned to one of the servers clearing the tables. "Do you think you could ask the young man who played Curly to come out to see us? I'd appreciate it."

"I can ask," she said and set down her tray, heading toward the stage door.

She returned, and Brit strode over a bit later in street clothes. Logan knew the second Brit recognized him by his radiant smile and the excitement in his eyes.

"Brit, this is Roger McAiry," Logan said.

Brit shook Roger's hand.

"I loved your performance. You have great timing, and you have incredible stage presence." Roger motioned to a chair.

Brit sat down across from them. "Thank you, but what's going on?"

Logan leaned closer. "Roger is a casting director. He's working on my next picture, and one of our supporting actors had to leave the cast because he broke his leg in Aspen last week."

"I saw your performance and the way you had the audience eating out of your hand the entire time." Roger finished his glass of sparkling water and set it on the table.

"You want me to audition?" Brit asked.

Roger shook his head. "I think I just saw a two-hour audition of amazing caliber. The part isn't huge, but it's a good one. You would be needed on set for about three weeks. Would that be something you'd be interested in?"

Brit gasped and put his hand over his mouth. "Are you kidding?" he asked, turning to Logan. "Is this a joke?"

Logan shook his head. "No. Roger is the real deal, and he knows how to spot talent." He grinned and didn't understand why Brit scowled.

"Sir, is this something you're doing because Logan asked you to? I don't want any favors. If this is a real offer because you like what I did, then yes. But if this is to make Logan happy somehow…."

Roger leaned over the table. "I just saw you in command of a half-drunk and laughing audience for two hours. No, this is not because Logan asked me to see you. He brought me here, but he didn't tell me anything else. You got this chance on your own." Roger stood up and handed Brit a card. "Text that number as soon as you can with your name, where I saw you, and how I can get in touch with you or your agent." He held out his hand, and Brit shook it.

"I don't have an agent," Brit said gently.

Roger chuckled. "Then get one. Use my name or Logan's. I'll have someone in touch with you tomorrow with the details." He smiled and turned toward the exit.

"Thank you," Brit said, clutching the business card like it was a lifeline.

"No, thank you. I have been looking for someone with just your look, build, and style for this role. And don't change a thing about your appearance. It's just what we want." Roger paused next to Logan. "I'll call a car and get a ride home." He patted Logan's shoulder once more. "This was a great evening." Then he left the theater.

"You really did this? Why?" Brit asked.

Logan shrugged. "I brought Roger to the theater for the evening. *You* were the one who won him over." He finished his drink and set the glass on the table. "Are you ready to go?"

"I'm done for the evening, but I can't leave my car here, and I don't want to ask the guys to drive it home for me again."

"Fine. Can you come to the house?" Logan asked. "I'll meet you there."

"I'm not far away," Brit countered. "Meet me here in half an hour so I can drop my car at home." He jotted down an address, and Logan took it. Then Brit kissed him on the cheek and hurried backstage once again.

Logan folded the paper and slipped it into his pocket. He called for his car and left the theater ten minutes later. He slid into the back of the limousine as soon as it stopped, and gave the driver the address, his heart pounding like he was seventeen again the entire ride to the address they were given.

Brit climbed into the back, settled next to him, and closed the door. "Is everything okay?" He nodded, his smile radiant. "Did you tell your friends?"

"No," Brit answered. "I don't want to jinx anything. I don't have the job until I have a contract… or some sort of details. Too many things fall through at the last minute."

"This won't." Logan handed Brit a glass. "You deserve to celebrate a little." He downed his own drink, and Brit took a few sips of his before setting it aside.

"Where are we going?" Brit looked out the window. "Can I see the script? Do you know which part he wants me for?" He was as excited and jumpy as a kid who'd just been given his first car.

Logan pulled him into an embrace. "Yes, to both. I thought we could get you something to eat if you're hungry."

Brit shook his head. "I can cook, maybe make you some real food." He settled against Logan, and things felt right with the world, at least for a few moments. That splintery feeling that seemed like such a regular part of him slipped away. Logan angled Brit's face upward and kissed him.

"You'd cook for me?" He wasn't sure what he had in the house besides protein drinks and stuff like that, but there had to be something. Carlton arranged to have things delivered, so anything was possible. It had been a long time since he'd eaten a meal that hadn't been delivered or from the table at a party or catered at a movie set.

Brit returned the kiss, pressing Logan back in the seat, heat and energy filling the small space. Unlike the night before, Brit didn't stop driving Logan out of his mind until they turned into the drive.

Brit slowly sat up, coloring deeply and straightening his clothes before getting out. Logan followed, a little wobbly on his legs as they walked to the door. Logan's mouth had been dry, but within seconds, his lips had moistened and he swallowed hard, because damn, the old jeans Brit wore hugged his backside like a glove.

"Are you watching my ass?" Brit asked, turning at the door with a leer.

Logan let them inside and enclosed Brit in his arms. "What if I was?"

Brit smiled and kissed him hard, tugging on his lower lip. "Okay. As long as you're honest about it." He kicked the door closed and pressed Logan against it.

Usually Logan was the one to take charge in these situations, but Brit definitely had other ideas. Damn, Brit was all energy, and Logan went with it until he pulled back.

"I think I promised to make you dinner," Brit whispered.

"We could eat later," Logan offered, trying to catch his breath and think straight. Not that he had a lot of luck in that department.

"I think we'd better eat now, because I'd say we're going to work off a whole lot of calories." Brit was as flushed as Logan felt, and Logan swallowed hard before nodding slowly. Something about Brit drew Logan. Maybe it was because he was real and there was no falsehood in him. Brit was the genuine article.

"Let me see what we have," Brit said as he checked out the refrigerator. "Eggs...." He started pulling things out. "How about a quiche?"

"Won't that take a while?"

Brit grinned. "Not if you help me. Though it will need to bake a while."

Logan had never cooked or baked in his life. He warmed stuff up or ordered in, but it seemed that Carlton kept the kitchen stocked. Brit put together the dough for a crust and got Logan involved mixing it. Then he rolled it, lined a glass pan he found, and put it in the oven. "We need to let the crust bake some first." He slid over some broccoli and had Logan cut it while Brit cooked small pieces of turkey bacon.

It seemed strange working in the kitchen at all, and yet Logan smiled whenever Brit bumped into him. "Logan," Carlton called as he came in the door. "You're cooking?" he asked as he came in. "Who's this?"

"Brit." Logan finished what he was doing. "What are you doing here this late?"

Carlton greeted Brit briefly, without losing focus. "I thought you might want to know about some of the early reviews." He climbed onto one of the stools. "They aren't great, but they aren't terrible either." He thumbed through his phone. "One reviewer says, 'There are glimpses of the Logan Steele I fell in love with in *Legion of Honor*, and I wish there was more of that spark.'"

Logan set the knife aside. "I see." He swallowed hard and went over to the bar while Brit continued cooking.

"There are others, and they liked the movie. So it isn't all bad. Just not what we had hoped," Carlton said. "You know this was problematic and that the chemistry with the rest of the cast was difficult. A number of the streaming services are interested in picking it up, so it's not going to be a washout, just not the mega-hit we were all hoping for." He set his phone aside as Logan poured a glass of whiskey and threw it back.

"Hey," Brit said as he came over. He gently set Logan's glass aside. "It's not the end of the world. You have another movie starting in a few weeks, and you'll make that one the best ever. Put all this behind you and concentrate on what's ahead." Brit took his hand. "Come on. You were helping me with something to eat." He gentled Logan back into the kitchen and took the crust out of the oven. "Go ahead and spread out the broccoli…. Now add the turkey bacon…." Once he was done, Brit poured over the liquid and carefully put the dish back in the oven and set the timer.

"You have him cooking. I can't believe it," Carlton told Brit, who had already started cleaning up.

"It will take about half an hour to bake." Brit put away the unused ingredients, wiped down the counter, and then stood next to Logan and leaned against his side. "Is there anything else you two need to talk about?" Brit asked, looking to Logan and then to Carlton.

"No. I thought…." Carlton slipped off the stool. "I think I'll head on out and leave you two to your dinner. Call me if you need anything. I'll get in touch when I hear something more, and I'll see you Monday." He tilted his head toward the front door, and Logan followed him to see Carlton out.

"What's going on?" Logan asked.

"Who is that guy? He was here last night, and now he's here again, cooking you dinner." Carlton narrowed his eyes. "Do you know what this guy wants? I already heard about Roger and his offer." He stepped closer. "What is it you think you're doing?"

Logan kept calm. "It's fine. Brit knew nothing about Roger. I brought him to the theater, and he liked what he saw. And as for what he's doing… Brit is cooking, and we're up to something decadently terrible here in Holly-wood. We're having dinner, and he's cooking it himself." Logan put his hand over his chest in fake drama.

"Fine. But what is he after?" Carlton asked. "You don't know this guy, and he doesn't seem like one of the usual hangers-on. Which worries me—I know how to deal with guys like that."

"He isn't like that at all. It's *why* I like him." Logan stood chest to chest with Carlton.

Carlton backed away. "You know I'm more than your manager. I'm also your friend, and I'm worried about you. If you want to date, then we can find you someone appropriate who understands how things work." Logan followed Carlton's glance to where Brit was checking on the quiche. "He's just after whatever you can do for him." Logan had never heard that much spite in his voice before.

Logan growled softly. "I don't think so, Carlton, and right now I'll be the one making the judgments and deciding who I want in my life." He opened the door. "Thank you for letting me know about the reviews, and we can go over my schedule for the next few days when I see you."

Carlton nodded, but he didn't step outside. "Just be careful, Logan." Now his tone was much gentler and more concerned. "There are lots of guys who would

love to be able to use you to get what they want, and I
don't want to see that happen." He clapped Logan on
the shoulder. "It's my job to watch out for you." The
intense expression in Carlton's eyes had Logan wondering if that was his only motive. "I've been with you
since the beginning, and I want to see you get to the
very top in this town." He smiled. "Just be careful."

He left, and Logan closed the door after him.

"So, we have another twenty minutes," Brit said
when Logan returned to the kitchen. "Whatever are we
going to do?" The glint in those eyes made Carlton's
warning zip right out of Logan's mind. He could so easily get lost in those eyes.

"I don't know. What do you want to do? I had a few
ideas last night, but you seemed to have other ones."
When he'd had guys over, this was about the time when
the two of them would get down to the fucking, so Logan was on new ground, and he found he liked it. "So
I don't want to presume anything." Still, anticipation
zipped through him, only adding to the moment.

Brit took his hand and tugged him closer. "Last
night you had just picked me up at the theater and
swept me off my feet. If I had stayed, I would have
been booted out in the morning and that would have
been that. But I didn't, and then you came to find me
and you brought company."

"So…?" Logan breathed.

Brit made lines up his arm with the tip of his finger.
"So you had to work to find me and put some effort
into it. If I made it too easy, you'd simply fuck me into
oblivion and then kick me out once the sun came up.
And now…."

Logan smiled. "And now I have no idea what you
want. I'm not a relationship kind of guy."

Brit chuckled and leaned even closer. "I don't think you have a clue what kind of man you are. I think you've been playing roles for so long that the real person inside this Logan Steele exterior has just gotten lost."

"I know reality from fiction," Logan said, straightening up. He should have been offended, but the more he thought about it, the more he knew Brit was probably right.

"Of course you do. But are you really Logan Steele or Wally Padgett from Loganville?" Brit asked. "Logan Steele is bigger than life, but I have a feeling that it was Wally Padgett who helped rescue my mother yesterday, and it was probably Wally who brought Roger to see the show. Logan Steele is nice to look at, and he cuts a mean figure on the big screen, but he isn't you. Not really."

Logan smiled. "I don't know if anything is that simple." He wasn't that deep a thinker.

"Sure it is." Brit grinned and closed the distance between them. "The Hollywood guy is Logan, but the guy underneath all that? He's the one I think I really like." Brit kissed him just as the timer dinged. They pulled apart.

"I always wanted to hear bells," Brit quipped, and Logan rolled his eyes. "Let me pull this out. It can cool a little bit before we eat it." He took the dish out of the oven and set it on one of the burners. Logan grabbed a bottle of champagne and a couple of glasses.

"I thought we could eat out by the pool." He carried the bottle and glasses out and set them on one of the side tables near the lounges. When he returned, Brit had set out plates and forks. He cut slices of the quiche and handed Logan one.

"I really hope you like it," Brit said as he followed him out to the pool. They took their seats, and Logan popped open the bottle and poured them each a glass. He handed one to Brit.

"This is so good," Logan whispered as he took his first bite. The egg custard was light and fluffy, the bacon a little smoky, and the broccoli had a little crunch. He turned to Brit, who smiled back at him.

"I probably should have added a little onion," Brit said.

Logan leaned over the space between them. "Who wants onion breath to do this?" He set his plate on the cushion and drew Brit into a kiss. Brit put his plate down too, and Logan slipped his hand around the back of Brit's neck and held him in place just so he could feast on those luscious lips.

The chair squeaked a little as Logan shifted his weight. Then he pulled back, and Brit held his gaze. There was something rich in those deep blue eyes that touched Logan deep inside. He wasn't sure what it was or why, but he wanted to get closer to Brit, spend time with him, and dammit, he was so hot for the guy he could barely think at all.

Brit picked up his plate and took another bite, holding Logan's attention. He got his own plate and ate slowly without breaking the gaze between them. Looking away seemed impossible, and he finished the quiche without taking his eyes off Brit. Then, once again, he set the plate aside. Every time that fork slipped between Brit's lips, Logan wanted to lean closer and suck the upper one between his. He had never considered eating an erotic activity, but Brit sure as hell made it seem that way, and Logan was certain he wasn't trying. Maybe he was just being that wildly driven out of his mind.

Logan drank his champagne and refilled his glass, drank that as well, and poured a third before topping off Brit's. He drank some more and reached for the bottle, but Brit put it aside. "There's no need for that," he said gently.

"I like it."

"I know. But you don't need to drink so much. I want you to remember everything about tonight." He set his plate aside and brushed Logan's hair away from his eyes. "I honestly don't know how much time we have together. You're Logan Steele, a huge celebrity. We come from different worlds, and I don't know if it's possible to bridge something like that."

"Brit... I—" Logan began, but Brit pressed a finger to his lips.

"Don't say anything or make promises you can't keep. Because I know the situation, and I'm going into it with my eyes open." He shifted closer. "We have whatever time we have, and you and I have to make the most of it." Brit finished his champagne and then stood. The water in the pool sparkled behind him as he toed off his shoes and then opened the buttons of his shirt. He dropped it on the lounger and turned around before slipping his pants down his legs to pool on the concrete. Then Brit walked to the edge of the water and dove in, barely making a splash.

Logan watched Brit glide through the water with effortless grace, barely coming up for air before slipping under the water once more. He was so beautiful, and Logan sat still, just watching for a while, before he too slipped out of his clothes and descended the stairs. The water was waist-deep as Brit surfaced just in front of him like an ancient water god, droplets sliding down his smooth chest to rejoin their brethren.

Brit stood still, his hair plastered to his head, eyes bright, and Logan closed the distance between them and wrapped his arms around Brit, who kissed him hard, tugging Logan forward.

They both tumbled into the water, kissing as it closed over their heads, blocking out everything until they surfaced together in each other's arms. Logan couldn't seem to get away, not that he wanted to for a second. He managed to tug them to the shallow area of the pool and held Brit as he pressed him against the side. "I don't want to let you go." There was something in Brit that he needed, but he had no idea what it was or why.

"Then don't," Brit whispered back. "Hold me like this forever. The rest of the world can exist out there beyond that tall hedge and fence. Bad things and stupid opinions can hold sway there, but in here, it's just the two of us."

Logan closed his arms around him, and Brit lifted his legs and wrapped them around Logan's waist.

Logan supported Brit's amazing ass and kissed him hard, moving slowly through the water until he reached the steps. Logan rested Brit back, his body in the water, cock sticking out, and damned if he didn't lean forward and take as much of him as he could.

Brit quivered, making ripples in the water, groaning softly in the night air. He tasted salty sweet, ambrosia as far as Logan was concerned. He wanted to drive Brit crazy. Brit's head lolled back and his legs stretched out. Logan lifted him in his hands, letting the water support Brit, taking him all the damned way.

Logan had always loved the sounds of the night, but these—Brit in the throes of ecstasy, unable to contain himself, lying back and gasping softly—were almost too much. He wanted this man in every way possible, and yet he was afraid to take him. This needed to last, so Logan backed off and took a deep breath, watching as Brit's chest rose and fell in heaving breaths.

"Jesus...."

"Never been sucked off by a movie star before?" Logan quipped.

Brit drew Logan within inches of his face. "I got news for you. Logan Steele disappeared with those clothes. I'm here with Wally, the man under the clothes and the image." He held Logan still. "I see you for who you really are… or at least part of who you are. It isn't the movie star or the celebrity who's here with me. Not tonight. It's just you." He closed the distance between them, and Logan realized that Brit had just said the sexiest words he had ever heard.

Logan wondered how long it had been since someone had actually seen him and not some image or mask that he let them see. He had buried himself so far under his persona that he was in danger of getting lost completely.

"I think before both of us get too cold, we should head inside. The pool is really nice, but the tile and concrete aren't anywhere near as comfortable as the huge bed I bet you have upstairs." Brit pressed to him, kissed him once more, and then turned and climbed out of the pool, giving Logan one hell of a show.

Logan followed him out and went to the pool house, where he grabbed a pair of robes before handing one to Brit. They brought in the dishes and glassware and set them on the counter. Then Logan took Brit's hand and led him up the stairs, turning out the lights as he went.

By the time they reached the bedroom, Logan was on fire. He slipped off his robe and tackled Brit onto the mattress, his control slipping away as they tumbled into hours of passion.

CHAPTER 4

BRIT DID his best to concentrate over the next couple days, but he found it hard, especially now that he was on set watching three guys go at it for two hours. Though he had to admit, it was mechanical and nothing at all like his night with Logan. Still, he did his job and was happy once the day was over and he could head home.

Brit hadn't heard from Logan, other than a few text messages. He was busy with the talk shows and even had a *Late Night* appearance last night. Brit had stayed up just to watch. Logan had done well, but there had been something a little off. No one else probably would have noticed it, and Logan had been funny and upbeat, but Brit couldn't help wondering if Logan had been drinking too much. He wondered if maybe he had taken something to either perk him up or to settle him down. Brit knew things like that happened all the damned time, and he hated to think of it happening to Logan.

I saw the reviews for Knockout, and some people weren't kind, Clive messaged. Brit had dragged his friend to see it just so he could watch the film himself. The movie wasn't bad by any means, but it wasn't great either.

I know, he messaged back. *I thought of putting something up myself, but no one is going to listen to me, and I don't need it to come out since I've been seeing him.* Brit hated that Logan was having a difficult time right now.

Is he doing okay? Clive asked.

Brit wished he knew. He sent Logan another message and got a reply that he was at home. *I don't know. Trying to find out,* Brit sent to Clive. *Talk to you later.* Then he switched to Logan. *I'm almost done with work. Last show was last night.*

Want to review the script? Logan asked, and Brit messaged that he could be there in an hour. At least he'd see Logan in person.

Brit put his phone in his pocket and gathered his things. He hoped that he would be able to let this particular job fade into the rearview mirror of his life sooner rather than later. After recording some "dialogue" to overdub, Brit hightailed it out of there and down the freeway to Bel Air. The gate at Logan's house slid open. He pulled in and got out of his car. He reached the door as Logan opened it, glass in hand.

Brit went inside and gave Logan a kiss that seared all the way to Brit's toes. "How are you doing?" he asked. "I went to see the movie."

Logan shook his head. "It was terrible, I know." He lowered his head, looking at the floor. "I read some of the reviews." He sighed and raised his glass.

Brit placed his hand on Logan's arm. "It wasn't terrible by any means, and there were some moments when I laughed. At times I could see you coming out and shining through. The script kind of fell flat." He took the glass as well as Logan's hand and led him through to the sitting room that overlooked the amazing backyard and pool.

"Thank you for saying that, but I know it's not true. At least not entirely." Logan reached for his glass. Brit wished he could stop him. He had already been drinking—Brit had smelled it on his breath.

Brit took the bottle before Logan could pour and placed it back on the bar. Logan flashed him a hard look, and Brit gave him one right back. "That isn't helping," Brit snapped. "You need to be able to think and stop burying yourself." He stroked Logan's cheek. "Let out the man I know is inside you and stop trying to bury him." Brit kissed him hard, and Logan held him close. Brit was under no illusion that his few words were going to change Logan, but he hoped that a message of hope and care would get through.

"Did you eat?" Logan asked once he broke the kiss. "I had some things delivered that my trainer recommended."

Brit went to the refrigerator and began pulling out things for a large salad.

"There's no-fat dressing and…."

Brit made a face. "That stuff is so full of salt and chemicals." He began getting out other things and whipped up a dressing of his own after he got Logan cutting up vegetables, chicken, and turkey.

"You know, I could hire a chef to do all this," Logan said as he nearly cut his finger.

Brit took the knife and had him tear up lettuce instead. "Where's the fun in that?" He bumped Logan's hip. "Having people do everything for you only means that you have more time to sit around and worry. I like to keep busy."

"What do you have to worry about?" Logan asked.

Brit snorted. "This movie part, where they got back to me and they're sending a contract. But I don't know the first thing about that stuff. See? Worry." He finished the dressing and put the bottle in the refrigerator to sit.

"Let me message my agent, Archie Millard, and see if he'll take you on as well." Logan grabbed his phone, sent a message, and got a response right away. "He says he'll meet you tomorrow. I sent him your phone number." Sure enough, Brit's phone chimed with a message, and Brit answered, providing quick details and setting up a time to speak. "That's one worry down."

"Yeah. The rest is just things like making rent, paying for gas, being able to stop being the porn voice-over guy, and maybe figuring out what the hell I'm going to do for a job that lasts more than a few weeks." He didn't bring up the worry he carried around for Logan and this damned movie.

Logan's phone vibrated on the counter, and he punched the speaker button.

Brit continued working but said nothing, wondering if he should leave the room. Yet Logan could have taken the call privately if he'd wanted to. "What's up, Carlton?"

"Just checking to see if you needed anything. I know it's been a tough day," Carlton said. He sounded sincere, but Brit didn't like the guy, and he wasn't sure why. There had been something in the way Carlton had looked at Logan and then at him with such icy chill. Maybe the guy had resting ice-man face. Without understanding it,

Brit found himself tensing as soon as he heard his voice. "I could come over if you want to talk or something."

Logan stilled. "No, I'm fine," he said, sharing a smile with Brit. "I know I have another appearance tomorrow and a trainer appointment, so I'll be ready. I'm sitting here chilling, and I think I just want to be left alone tonight."

"Okay. But if you're having a tough time, I put something to help you relax on the nightstand next to your bed in the little plastic case. Get some rest and try to relax. We'll take another stab at it tomorrow."

Logan ended the call and set the phone aside.

Brit shook his head. The guy Carlton was a real piece of work. Instead of helping Logan through this tough time, he seemed to talk in such a way as to guarantee that Logan would be worried—it was like he was trying to wind him up. And Brit could see it in Logan's eyes and the way he drummed his fingers on the counter. He had been relaxed before that fucking call, and now he was a bundle of nerves.

"Can you get out a couple of bowls?" he asked gently. When Logan turned around, he ran his hand lightly up and down Logan's back. Logan leaned into the touch, stopping what he was doing and just standing still. Brit said nothing and let his hands to the talking, only letting them slip away when Logan moved to get the bowls. "Thanks. Do you want to get the script and we can go over it while we eat?"

Logan went down the hall, and Brit dressed the salads and took them to the table. He brought them each a soda and set everything out so when Logan returned, they could sit down.

Logan handed Brit the opened script and took his place. "This is where your character comes in."

Brit took a bite, chewing as he read over the part. It wasn't a huge part, but Brit saw humor in the words and smiled. As he read on, the character began to take shape in his mind. He handed the script to Logan.

"Do you want to read it together?"

"I got it," Brit said, leaning closer. "I see this going one of two ways. I could play the character straight, but that would be kind of boring. Ambrose is supposed to be your character, Simon's onetime nemesis, now turned friend of a sort."

"Exactly. They have a history, but the situation has changed their relationship, and in the end, it's Ambrose who makes the sacrifice so Simon can defuse the bomb and save the city from annihilation. So it's a good part, even if it isn't a huge one." Logan smiled and began reading lines.

Brit read his lines, reacting as best he could to what Logan was saying. Brit made a face. "I know what the character is, but I'm not getting him."

Logan nodded and took a few bites of his dinner. "It's flat. Let's try again."

Brit knew he was right and took another bite, trying to get his mind where it needed to be. In the theater, he had time to really work on his character with multiple rehearsals. He wasn't going to have that here. Someone might work with him on the part, but he was going to have to be prepared and come in full bore right from the start. This was his one chance, and he had to make the most of it or there wasn't going to be a second one. Brit felt some of the pressure Logan was under. But his was a small part, whereas Logan was expected to carry the damned movie.

Brit read through it again, this time trying harder to get the character in his head. "It's not right, and I'm coming off weird." He pushed the script away and ate a little more, trying to think. He appreciated that Logan didn't push him, and he placed his hand on Logan's, who turned his over. Brit interlocked their fingers. He was tempted to push the script and the food aside, straddle Logan's lap right there, and ride him for all he was worth. He had been thinking about the stunning man all day, but they had work to do.

"You need to make this character yours somehow," Logan said. "They're just words on the page otherwise."

"Okay. I get that. But what if we make the guy funny? There's plenty here to play with." He pointed to one section. "Not play him queeny, but quippy. Instead of saying the lines, what if he tosses them off, almost over his shoulder. I mean, Simon is you, so he's big and strong, the hero standing on top of the world with his hair flying in the breeze, and Ambrose can be the guy who farts into your breeze, so to speak. It would make him memorable, even if he's only on-screen for ten minutes at most."

Logan read through the lines, and Brit delivered his, sinking into the character almost immediately. He easily tossed off his lines as written, but he added enough camp to give them a second meaning. It was funny and interesting, and Logan beamed at him. "I knew as soon as I saw you on stage that first time that you had something special." He sipped from the glass and drew Brit closer, kissing him with all the excitement of the moment.

Then he pulled back and took a bite before whispering. "Sometimes I wish I still had that."

Brit smacked the table, rattling the dishes and startling Logan. "You fucking do," he snapped. "Look at

this. You have great lines. Your character is a strong
hero, but right here, with Ambrose, we get to see that
part of it, at least, is an act. Let some of the hurt and
anxiety you're feeling right now show through in that
scene. Put yourself into this character." He stabbed at
the pages with his finger. "I know you can do this because I've seen you do it before."

Logan sighed. "I know. This used to be so easy, but
now I have no idea what I'm doing most of the time.
What just came to me before has turned into trying to
figure out how not to suck." He sounded so lost.

"First thing, you don't suck. My drama teacher in
high school once told me that if you go on stage and
worry about sucking or not being good, then you'll
fail." Brit realized he needed to try to help Logan, if
Logan would let him. "So how do you see yourself
playing Simon? How do *you* see Simon?"

Logan ate a few bites of his salad, and Brit did as
well. "I mean…," he began and fell apart. "He's the
hero, and I was going to play him as one. Big, strong,
the one who saves everything."

"Yeah, he is that. But what is he scared of? What
does he want? What makes him a really good hero?
It isn't that he's perfect, but that he has flaws, and if
they aren't written in the script, then you have to give
him some. Make him hesitate at the right moments
and maybe even be unsure of himself. All good heroes
overcome the situation they're presented with and their
own inner demons." Brit set the script aside and finished his salad. Then he cleaned up and let Logan finish
before grabbing the script.

"Where are you going?" Logan asked once Brit
had cleared his dishes.

"The movie opens in an office, so we're going to your office." Brit led the way and used the printer/copier inside to make a copy of the first part of the script. "Now, let's go through this and see if we can figure it out and start to get you in the right space." He collected the copies and then sat down, giving Logan the full script. "Does anyone do a read-through with you?"

"Carlton used to, but he's gotten busier, and…." Logan shrugged, and Brit's dislike for the man grew a little more. Everyone needed someone to support them, and it sounded like Logan didn't have that.

"Then we can work together," Brit told him. "Now, let's read through this first part and see if anything comes to you."

He hurried to the kitchen and returned with a couple bottles of water. He handed Logan one and then settled into one of the comfy chairs.

BRIT AND Logan reviewed the script until nearly midnight. What surprised Brit was how Logan had great ideas for his character but seemed stymied by his own role. They continued working until Logan started fleshing out the character and Brit's head was about ready to split in two. All evening he had been in the office with Logan, his scent growing more intense as time passed, and he'd had to work harder and harder to keep his concentration on the task rather than jumping Logan where he sat. The impulse popped into his mind about every ten minutes. Logan's ideas sounded good to him, and they continued working through the script until Brit could no longer keep his eyes open.

"I should probably go home," he whispered, setting aside the copies of the script that he'd been using.

"Let's go up to bed," Logan replied. He lowered his legs from the footstool and slowly got to his feet.

Brit agreed and followed him up the stairs, turning out the lights as they went.

When they entered the bedroom, Brit watched as Logan picked up the little plastic pill container by the side of the bed. Brit came up behind him and slid his arms around his waist. "You don't need that."

Logan turned around in his arms. "I never sleep very well."

Brit slid his hand down Logan's arm. "You certainly didn't need it the other night, and you won't need it now." He hated that Carlton had placed the damned thing there. The guy was really starting to get on Brit's nerves. He was Logan's manager and was supposed to be helping him, not pushing pills. Brit was starting to wonder about the kind of support Logan had around him. "Try putting it aside and coming to bed."

Logan set the container back on the table. "It's been a long time since I was really able to sleep on my own."

Brit pressed Logan down onto the bed. "You know, I can give you something that's a lot better than a sleeping pill. That's for damned sure." He smiled and slipped his hands under Logan's shirt, pushing the fabric upward. Brit wanted as much of Logan as he could get. The past few hours had taxed his concentration to the max, and now it was just the two of them, no scripts or work.

"I don't know why I can't seem to get you out of my head," Logan said as Brit let his hands wander. Logan was strong, fit, and sexy as all hell.

"Do you want to?" Brit asked, and Logan shook his head slowly. "Then why worry about it?" He was coming to understand that something about Logan Steele got under his skin too. It frightened him, because he kept wondering when Logan was going to wake up and realize Brit was a nobody, just some guy he'd helped at an accident. But damn, he was here right now, and the way Logan reacted to him sent Brit's heart soaring.

Logan's eyes were wide and huge. Brit had no illusions that Logan had tried more than once to live better through chemistry in one way or another, but this reaction was all because of him. His breath came in slow pants, which only revved Brit even more.

He pushed Logan's shirt off, hands shaking a little because every touch seemed extraordinary and he didn't want any of this to end. Yet he was pretty sure that at some point Logan was going to realize just how ordinary Brit was, and all Brit would be left with were his memories.

Logan sat up. "Now who's thinking too much?" He cupped Brit's cheeks. Brit hadn't even realized that he'd gone stock-still, sinking into his own thoughts.

"I'm sorry." Brit lay on the bed next to Logan and wondered what the hell was getting into him. He was usually really focused, and now, when he tried to think, his mind kept circling back to Logan. Not that it was a bad thing, but it was like every now and then it all short-circuited.

Logan slid off the bed and took Brit's hand, tugged him off the sheets, and then led him down the stairs. They went out back, the lights off. Brit expected Logan to take him to the pool, its black void just catching a little light on the surface. Instead, Logan turned right along the walk and out toward the pool house. He slid open a door and flipped a switch, and a jacuzzi with jets everywhere came to life.

Logan slipped off his pants and slowly stepped into the water, long cock pointing toward the ceiling when he turned. His heated gaze raked over Brit, and Brit took off his shirt without thinking, the rest of his clothes following in a blur, like he was under a spell. If that were true, then Brit would stay with him forever. He descended the steps into the water and went right into Logan's arms, pressing his hands to Logan's chest. He was hotter than the water around them as Brit feasted on Logan's lips, sucking on his tongue and taking all he could get.

Something inside his mind flipped on, and he slid his hand down Logan's belly and wrapped his fingers around Logan's length, holding fast. He needed more of this man.

"Hell…. Brit…." Logan's whimper reached his ears, sending Brit even higher. He wanted to make Logan happy, to give him something to remember when things got tough. Logan quivered in his embrace, and Brit lowered the intensity a little, not wanting things to end too soon. They had all the time they wanted.

Brit pressed Logan against the tiles at the side of the whirlpool, holding him in place. He couldn't get enough of Logan and probably never would. That was the kicker.

"What are you thinking?" Logan whispered.

"That you're going to realize how ordinary I am at any moment." Brit blinked into Logan's intense eyes and kissed him hard before he could say anything. Brit didn't want anything to intrude on this moment. If it was an illusion or him letting his feelings race away with him, he didn't want to know, at least not now. He could stick with that illusion for a little while.

Logan cupped his cheeks. "You aren't ordinary." He held Brit's face in his hands and looked deep into him. "Brit Stevens, you're something way beyond that." Logan kissed him and lowered them both. The water that swirled around them only increased the desire that coursed through Brit with the force of a jet engine. He slipped a leg between Logan's, bringing their hips together, pressing his chest to Logan's for all the contact he could possibly get. Any space between them seemed way too much, and Brit clutched Logan to him. It surprised him that Logan seemed to feel the same way. Every time the water pushed them away from each other, they came back together, needing each other even more than before. "I want you forever...."

Brit shook in the heat, and Logan lifted him out of the water and onto the side, then pressed him back against the tile. He took Brit between his lips, sinking down around him, stealing Brit's ability to breathe. "Fucking God," Brit groaned. "Don't stop." He carded his fingers through Logan's thick hair, needing contact as Logan threatened to suck his brains out. "Jesus... fuuuuccckkkk," he groaned. His hands shook and his mouth ran away with him. It was like he lost control of everything he was saying, and he didn't care in the least.

After a few seconds he heard himself and snapped his mouth shut. He sounded like one of those damned voice-overs he did almost every single day.

Logan pulled away, Brit's cock slapping against his belly. "That was something."

Brit felt himself blushing. "I never told you, but I pay the rent working on adult films." He sat up. "Not in them, but I work as crew and stuff."

Logan chuckled. "I knew you had hidden talents." Damn, the man didn't even bat an eyelash. "Let's see what you've got." He kissed Brit and then held his gaze for a second before taking Brit all the way in a single movement.

"Fucking hell," Brit ground out as he barely managed to keep control of himself and not lose it in a matter of seconds. "Yeah... oh my God...."

Logan chuckled as he kept it up. The cool tiles were the only thing keeping Brit from overheating, and when Logan lifted his legs and teased him with his fingers, he nearly came unglued. It was almost too much—his cock down Logan's throat, fingers at his entrance, teasing, lightly probing... he needed so bad.

"You keep taking your fucking time," Brit growled.

"And I'm going to," Logan said, shooting water at him and then blowing on his wet skin, sending shivers through him. Brit shook on the tile and clamped his eyes closed because watching was almost unbearable. He could only take so much, and his mind was about to fry like the time he'd plugged in the toaster wrong as a kid. He gave over to Logan until his lips slipped away, and he looked up to see Logan hurrying across the pool area.

"What's going on?" It was like he had come out of a lust haze, blinking and wondering what the hell was happening. Logan returned, and Brit narrowed his gaze. "How often do you have guys in here?"

Logan had a condom and set it next to him. "You're the first. This has always been my place to go and relax. I keep this closed even when people come over." He leaned over him. "These are here for when the guys get... a little busy."

Brit wound his arms around Logan's neck. "You better not have any use for them with anyone other than me." He actually growled, feeling possessive as all hell.

Logan drew closer. "I don't think I knew what having someone in my life was like until you." He kissed Brit again, and Brit's heart warmed, even if he wasn't ready to fully believe it yet. They hadn't known each other that long, and Logan's life was in such flux. Hell, his own was in for monumental changes as well, and pronouncements made in the heat of passion were most definitely to be taken with a grain of salt.

Still, the way Logan looked at him, like he was the sun itself and everything revolved around him, was almost enough for Brit to put aside his natural skepticism and just go along with whatever Logan said. Hell, as Logan pressed to him, Brit held his breath and waited, willing to give Logan anything at that moment.

"Are you going to take all day?" he begged.

Logan pressed forward, and Brit opened to him, arching his back and moaning softly as the burn followed by pressure and stretch were replaced by mind-numbing pleasure that left him seeing double. Not that that was bad, considering it was two Logans, and the man was as hot as summer pavement. As Logan leaned over him, Brit basked in the water that glistened off his chest, running down his skin as he sank deeper into Brit, sending him on a wild ride that he hoped never came to an end. Logan seemed intent on taking his time, and Brit tugged him down.

"I'm not made of glass," Brit told him. "You don't need to be gentle and so careful. Just be yourself."

Logan's expression darkened, his eyes deepening as he wrapped his arms around Brit, driving him to heaven. Brit clutched Logan with everything he had just to hold them together. Logan was intense, and Brit loved every second of it. The sexiest part was how Logan's gaze never left him and how he reacted to Brit's breathing and each and every whimper. No one had ever been able to read him this way. It sent Brit over the moon, and he hoped he never came back down.

"I don't want to hurt you," Logan whispered.

Brit groaned and pulled Logan into a kiss, meeting each movement with one of his own. Logan glistened as the humidity grew around them, intensity building until neither of them could hold back any longer. Logan pushed Brit over the edge with Logan following right behind, the two of them collapsing on the tiles, worn out completely, Logan in Brit's arms, breathing like he'd just won a race.

Brit didn't move, just lying still with Logan on top of him. He gasped as their bodies disconnected. Only then did Logan back away far enough to take care of the condom. Then he gently guided Brit into the water, holding him and running a finger up and down his arm. Neither of them said a word. There was only the hum of the whirlpool motor, the water swirling around them. Just about the point where Brit felt like he was about to doze off, Logan shifted and helped him out of the water.

They walked together across the yard and up through the house to the bedroom. Logan guided him to the bed like Brit was the most precious thing in the world to him, and then before he knew it, Logan pulled up the covers and Brit closed his eyes. It was almost too much to hope for that his life could be this good and that he could be cared for this way. Brit soaked it in, knowing that with his luck, everything would fall apart eventually. Still, he shifted closer to Logan, inhaled his scent, and let sleep overtake him.

"HOW DID it go with Archie?" Logan asked as soon as Brit called after the meeting with his new agent.

"Really well. He got the offer and had already countered it on my behalf. They upped their amount, and we agreed. They're going to pay me what I make in, like, five months for three weeks' work." Brit could hardly believe it. "I talked the part over with him to get his advice, and he said the same thing you did—play it as animated and interesting as possible—so that's what I'm going to do. They want me to start next week."

"Me too," Logan said, and Brit could feel his nerves coming through the phone.

"I need to go to my mom's, and I was wondering if you might want to come with me." Maybe getting Logan out of the same environment would be good for him. He knew that his mom loved Logan Steele and would fangirl all over him.

Wind rushed past in the background. "If you like, I can have your mom picked up and you both can come here. It's a lovely day, and I'd really like to see her again."

"Okay. I can call her." His mother was going to have a fit when she found out that he was seeing Logan Steele and hadn't told her a thing about it. "But why not just come with us?"

Logan sighed. "I don't think I want to be recognized." He really sounded down. "*Knockout* is being pulled from some theaters early, and I keep getting questions about what happened to me. Online, it's not pretty, and the attendance in theaters is drying up. Carlton thinks it's best if I stick close to home right now. He's been here most of the day."

Brit rolled his eyes. At least that explained the depression. He didn't think Carlton was good for Logan, but it wasn't his place to say anything. There was some weird dynamic going on there, though he couldn't put his finger on it. He wondered if Carlton had a thing for Logan or if the guy just wanted Logan to rely on him for everything. "Is he there now?"

"He left an hour ago," Logan said.

"Okay. Let me call Mom and let her know that a car will be picking her up, and if she's okay with that, then I'll meet you at the house as soon as I can." He ended the call and phoned his mom right away.

"When are you getting here? I was going to roast a chicken for dinner, but the ones at the store looked awful. So I got some wings and was going to bread and bake those." She sounded so excited—until she noticed Brit's silence. "Don't tell me you're not coming."

"Well…." Brit swallowed hard. "I was wondering if you might want to come out with me. A friend has asked me over for the evening, and he wondered if you'd like to come as well."

His mom hesitated. "What kind of friend is this?" She immediately perked up. "It isn't that Clive, is it? He's a nice man, but he would drive you crazy in a month. You're better off as a friend-friend with him rather than a boyfriend."

His mother had an opinion on everything and everyone. "No, Mom, I'm not talking about Clive. We are just friends and nothing more. I'm talking about a new friend… and I have some real news to share with you." He cleared his throat. "So do you want to come?"

"Sure. Should I bring the wings?" she asked.

"How about we let him cook, and you can make the wings another night? Though if you made your lemon cake, you might want to bring that." It was Brit's favorite, and she always made it for him when he came for dinner.

"Of course I did. Fine, I'll bring that. Are you on your way to pick me up?"

"No. My friend is sending a car to get you since I'm in a different area of the city. I'll meet you at his house."

"Brighton Stevens, what aren't you telling me?" He could just see her eyes narrowing in suspicion. "Since when do you have friends who send cars for people, and what is this surprise of yours?" That tone was the same one she'd used when he had been caught kissing Billy Webber in eleventh grade. Apparently his mother hadn't been upset he'd been kissing a boy—she just thought he could do better than Billy.

"Do you remember that nice man who rescued you from the car accident?"

His mother gasped. "You mean that hunky Logan Steele? Are you seeing him? Oh, honey, that man is sex on a stick. If he liked older women, I'd butter his bread eight ways from Sunday. I'd take hold of him and ride that man to hell and back again."

Brit sputtered and wondered how he was ever going to unhear that. "Please don't say something like that when you get to his house. Please. He came into the club a while ago, and, well… things have been pretty interesting. He invited you over for dinner." Brit pulled to the side in nearly stopped traffic and sent Logan a text with his mother's address and that she would love to come. The understatement of the year, apparently. He managed to get back out into the bumper-to-bumper traffic, willing it to move so he could get over and turn off at the next exit.

"Oh, sweetheart. He wants to meet your mother," she gushed, and he could practically see her rushing to her closet to try to figure out what to wear. "I need to get my face on and do something with my hair." She was already in a flutter.

"Just be ready." His phone vibrated, and he read the message from Logan. "The car will be there in thirty minutes. I'll be at Logan's and will see you there. Oh, and don't forget the cake." He grinned as she sputtered at him before disconnecting.

Brit got off the freeway and down onto Wilshire, then took the drive through Beverly Hills to Bel Air and made the turn into Logan's drive as a group of guys came down the sidewalk and turned up Logan's walk. They were either roving Abercrombie and Fitch guys willing to model for food, or a party.

"What's all this?" Brit asked Grant, who seemed like their leader.

"And you are?" He looked Brit over like he had just peed on his Guccis. The front door opened. "Logan!" the guy gushed. "We thought we'd bring a little fun your way."

Brit stifled a growl. Was Grant for real?

Logan turned to him and then to the group of hot guys in open shirts and some of the tiniest shorts known to man. "Grant, you should have called."

"It's been so quiet over here." Grant took off sunglasses that probably cost more than Brit made in a month. "We figured you must be in one of those hermit moods again and thought we'd cheer you up."

Brit turned back to his car. "It's okay." He wasn't going to stay if this was what Logan really wanted. Hell, he'd wait for his mom and just take her home. Though she'd probably get a kick out of the view, it wasn't something Brit was prepared for. He should have figured that whatever was happening with Logan had been his imagination and that Logan had a whole life Brit wasn't part of. It wasn't like Brit was against a good time. All he had to do was look over these half-dozen shaved, plucked, tanned, toned, and highlighted guys to see that there was no way he could measure up to that.

"I have plans for this evening," Logan said forcefully.

Grant approached him. "Come on, Logan. You never turned down a chance to party before."

Logan looked at him and then shook his head. "Some other time."

Grant huffed. "That's something I've never heard." He glared at Brit before leading the pack of guys back the way they'd come. He paused at the end of the property, giving Brit a final dirty look, and then the parade of guys disappeared down the walk.

"How often does something like that happen?" Brit asked as he approached the door.

Logan held a glass in his hand, and he motioned Brit inside and closed the door. "I don't know. Every now and then Grant drops by with a group of guys for some time by the pool." He made it sound like it was no big deal as Brit settled in one of the chairs.

"You don't invite them? They just show up?" That seemed rude to him and like they were taking advantage. Brit didn't know what went on at these parties, and he really didn't want to. It was obvious that Logan's life was a lot different from the one Brit led—that was for damned sure. "Is that the kind of thing you want?"

Logan shrugged. "It's hard to make real friends. The guys come over, spend an afternoon, and we have some fun. Then when the sun goes down, they tend to head off to the clubs or things like that." He sat down next to Brit. "After one of those parties, we ended up at your theater." He slipped closer. "I like to have a good time every now and then."

Brit got that, and he wasn't surprised. He figured that if he hadn't been here, Logan would probably have let those guys in and they would have settled into whatever kind of fun they usually had. The thought sent a jealous streak half a mile wide running through Brit. None of those guys gave a damn about Logan. All they cared about was having a good time, maybe sharing some selfies, drinking all of Logan's liquor, and getting busy in the pool house. "And exactly what kind of a good time do you have with them?" He glared at Logan. "I can imagine the kinds of things the muscle parade would be interested in."

Logan drank the rest of what was in his glass. "I sent them away." He set the tumbler on the counter.

"This time. But what about the next?" Brit met Logan's gaze. "What is it you want, and what am I to you?" He wouldn't let Logan squirm out of this. He felt like a fool. He had thought Logan really cared, but all it took was some guys wagging their asses at him and he was off in party fantasyland, with Brit standing on the outside looking in.

Logan stormed over to the bar and snatched up a bottle.

"Is that what you really want? To sit around here and get drunk?"

"Fuck you," Logan snapped.

"Yeah, well, you already did that... more than once." Brit held Logan's gaze and closed the distance between them. He hated the thought of those guys taking advantage of Logan. Maybe he let that feeling get the better of him. "Is that all I was to you? Just a quick fuck?" He didn't look away, and slowly Logan lowered his arms, taking the bottle along with them.

"No," he whispered.

"Then why act like it? Are you afraid that you might actually care for someone? Because the swimsuit brigade out there will be happy to come back. I'm sure they'll keep you happy for a few hours, and you can drink and forget about how alone you are. I bet if you called Carlton, he'd come over and gladly shake his dress-panted ass in front of you. Hell, he'd wave that thing like a flag if it got your attention." Brit was on a roll.

Logan glared at him for a few more seconds. "You're full of shit, you know that?" He set the bottle back on the tray.

"No, I'm not."

Logan shook his head. "Carlton?" He snickered. "Get real."

Brit sighed. "If you say so. But I see what I see." He closed the distance between the two of them. "You're the one with something to offer. Those hangers-on don't give a shit about you, and you know it. So why go along with what Grant or anyone else wants?"

"They're my friends," Logan answered, and his phone chimed. He looked at it and then at Brit. He suddenly seemed tired, like he understood exactly what Brit was concerned about but wasn't sure what to do about it. "The car is here."

Brit sighed because their timing was for shit. He and Logan were finally talking about something meaningful, and he'd hoped that maybe he could get Logan to tell him what it was that made him feel so worthless and why he thought he needed people like that in his life.

"Okay." Brit took Logan's hand, not sure what to say or how to end their disagreement. They hadn't solved anything or talked things out. He wasn't even sure Logan understood anything Brit had been trying to say.

"I can't spend my entire life alone," Logan added, looking forlorn, like his whole life was weighing on him.

"I know. And I don't want you to." Brit held his gaze, knowing that for Logan, finding real friends and people who would care about him for who he was had to be difficult. "Instead of people using you for their own gain, you can surround yourself with people who really care about you."

Maybe that was more than he should have said. Logan looked like he was going to argue, but then he shrank back a little, which worried Brit even more. If Logan fought with him, at least he'd know what the guy was thinking. But as it was, he got no information whatsoever.

"Like you?" Logan asked.

Brit chuckled. "Look at it this way. I care enough to argue and fight with you because I hate to see people taking advantage. And I want you to be happy. That's something I'm willing to fight for, so with all the humility I can muster at the moment, which isn't much, then yes, like me." He smiled to try to lighten things up. Everything he'd said was true. He also hated the thought of the Speedo brigade worming their way into Logan's affection and possibly his bed. So help him, just the thought of that made him want to claw their eyes out.

The doorbell sounded, and then the door opened and Brit's mom came inside, carrying a glass dish. Brit hurried over and took it, then guided her back to the room with the view of the backyard. "You remember Logan," Brit said. "This is my mother, Cynthia."

His mother beamed. "Of course I do." She came right over and kissed him on the cheek. "You're a hero, young man."

Logan suddenly seemed shy. "I don't know about that. But I'm so glad I could help you."

Mom laughed. "Help me? Young man, you made my week—heck, maybe my year. It isn't every day that you get pulled from an accident by a real-life star."

"Okay, Mom. That's enough gushing." Brit set the cake on the counter. "Mom brought her famous lemon cake, but just so you know, Logan and I have to be careful about what we eat because the camera really does add ten pounds." He beamed, and his mom put her hands to her cheeks.

"You got a part?" she practically screamed.

"Yes. We start filming next week. Logan is the star of the picture, but I have a really good part. It's only three weeks, but this is my chance." Brit took Logan's arm.

Mom glowered at both of them. "You didn't…," she began and then paused, losing her words.

"No, he didn't. My friend saw the show and was captivated. All I did was bring him to see Brit. He did the rest." Logan rolled his eyes. "I can see where Brit gets his skepticism and backbone from."

"And I watched your new movie," Cynthia told Logan. "It was pretty good." She leaned close. "Was that really your bare backside, or did they use a double?"

Logan chuckled. "I'll have you know that what you saw on-screen was all me." Brit already knew that was true.

Mom patted Brit on the shoulder. "Sweetheart, you're a lucky man." She looked wistful. "Your father had a backside you could bounce a quarter off of." She sighed. "Sometimes I miss that man some-thing fierce. Then I shake myself and get on with it."

"Mom," Brit said gently.

"I know. Your father is gone and on to his newer model, and the last time I saw him there was little left of the man I married." She stroked his cheek. "You know, what makes it hard is that since I don't see the old goat all that often, he stays young in my mind. Which really kind of sucks as I get older."

Logan offered her a chair, and she sat down. Brit helped with drinks and got a few snacks out of the re-frigerator. He had already learned that he knew more about what Logan had on hand than he did. "Can I ask if you liked the movie?"

Mom nodded. "It was pretty good, but I have to tell you that you made me cry in *Sunset*. Every time I watch that damned thing, I reach for the tissues. You should do more movies like that. I know the young people are into the action films, but you showed such emotion and care in that movie." She sighed, and Brit wished he could argue with her, but he had to agree. *Sunset* was Logan's best work, and it had been six years ago.

Logan sat heavily. "I wish I could get that back. But I don't know if I have it in me."

Brit handed him a glass of water and set down a tray of cheese, crackers, and fruit before perching on the wide arm of Logan's chair.

Brit took Logan's hand. "I know you do." He nudged Logan gently. "You showed the kind of care and who Logan Steele really is when you helped me and Mom at that accident. You didn't think of yourself, you just helped us, and you did it without thinking." Lo-gan nodded gently. "So if you aren't happy with what you're doing, put that into what we see on-screen." The lost look in Logan's eyes tugged at Brit's heart.

"Let's talk about something less depressing than the trajectory of my career," Logan said.

Brit wanted to argue, but a change of subject was probably a good idea.

"Tell me about this part you got," Brit's mom asked. "I'm so excited for you."

"It's not that big, but I think it's going to be fun."

"Is it a bad guy?" she probed. She loved her villains.

Logan leaned forward. "It's this great part. He plays the hero's sidekick... in a way. He's one of the characters with a huge heart, and in the end, he's the one who makes a sacrifice for the good of humanity. The way Brit wants to play the part is genius, because he'll add some humor to the movie."

"How exactly *did* you get this part?"

"Logan saw *Oklahomo!* with some friends." He was still not certain what kind of friends Grant and company were, but he wasn't going to bring that up right now. He couldn't live Logan's life for him. "He liked it and brought an associate to the next performance." Brit felt himself coloring a little.

"I recognized Brit on stage from earlier in the day, and I couldn't take my eyes off him. Afterwards, I invited him out, and one thing led to another." Mom narrowed her gaze.

"And I left Logan wanting more." Brit smirked.

"He didn't even leave his number."

Brit rolled his eyes. "Of course I didn't. You knew where I was going to be, and if you were interested, then I figured you could find me." He turned to his mom. "See, I learned from the best."

"What do you mean?"

Brit held Logan's gaze. "If I had stayed, then I would have been just another notch on your bedpost. I didn't want that. It's not the kind of guy I am. I don't know about you, but I'm looking for something special, meaningful." He waved his arm toward the backyard. "There's a city full of guys who would be more than happy to shtup their way into your bed and then be happy to go home and brag about it to all their friends. That isn't what I wanted." He swallowed hard. "And don't think I'm not aware that you've done plenty of that. So I figured if you had to extend a little effort and decide what you wanted, maybe I'd have a chance." He waggled his eyebrows. "And it worked. I know you brought Roger with you, but you came to see the show again because you were just fascinated by me." He batted his eyelashes like some demented Southern belle, and Logan leaned back in the chair, laughing. "And I was right, because I'm still here." Though he wondered how long Logan would want him to stick around. He was about to continue teasing Logan when something outside caught his ear.

"What is that?" Mom asked.

Logan already had his phone out.

Brit went to the windows in front and peered outside. "What the heck?" Three people walked up the drive past the gate, singing at the tops of their lungs. "Do you know these people?"

"Logan baby, come on out," one of them called loudly.

Logan groaned from behind Brit.

"We were so good together. I know you want some of this." The guy turned around, shaking his backside and nearly falling over in the process.

"Do you know who that is?" Brit asked as the guy in question led the other two around the side of the house. "He seems to know his way around." Brit sneered and walked through the house so he could look out into the backyard, where the guys stripped off their clothes and jumped naked into the pool.

"I have no idea who they are," Logan said quietly. The sad thing was that Brit didn't need to wonder if that were true. Apparently Logan's parties were legendary.

Logan got on the phone as he locked the exterior doors. "I have someone on their way to get them off the property." He set his phone aside while Brit closed the blinds. He hated the thought of the drunks seeing inside to him and his mother. "Excuse me a minute." Logan left the room.

"Is this something you want to be part of?" Brit's mom asked softly. "Has this happened before?"

"Not that I know of, but it wouldn't surprise me. I'm aware of Logan's past and his reputation, but he's always been good to me." The thing was that, like it or not, Logan Steele had worked his way into Brit's heart, and he was afraid there was no getting him out of it.

"Is that all there is?" She cocked her eyebrows. "Because if that's what this is, you're better off ending it now. You can find plenty of people who are good to you because you deserve it." She patted his knee.

Brit knew exactly where this was coming from, because the more he was around Logan, the more shades of his father seemed to come forward sometimes, and it worried him. Brit would be a fool if it didn't.

"I may have been joking about your father, but you know what he put us both through. Are you sure you want to go through that?" She held his gaze with her best mama bear expression. "I know this may not be what you want to hear, but…."

"I know, Mom, and it worries me. I know I can't fix him. That's something that's out of my control. But I care about him, and he's alone, flapping in the wind, with people like those guys around him." God, maybe he was just being the stupidest person on earth right about now and getting involved with Logan was the dumbest thing he had ever done. He had always hoped for doors to open, and they had.

Logan had helped with that, and Brit was grateful. He really was. He also knew that the things he felt for Logan weren't rooted in gratitude. He saw Logan's heart. Maybe others didn't, but he'd seen it when Logan had rescued his mother, and he'd seen it when he brought Roger to the show. And then there were the times at night when the house was quiet and it was only the two of them. Logan treated him like Brit was the center of the whole universe. Other than his mother, no one had done that before.

"All I can tell you, Mom, is that I'm in this with my eyes open. I know he has issues and there are things we need to talk about. And we will. I don't know if this is going to lead to anything, and it scares me sometimes…."

His mom nodded. "I know it does. And it's obvious what you feel for him." She leaned forward and hugged him. "I'm a mother, and I never want to see you get hurt. There's not a damned thing I can do about it, though. All I can ask is that you follow your heart."

Brit wiped the dampness from the corners of his eyes. "Thanks, Mom. But I'm afraid I've done that already." His throat ached, and he turned to look where Logan had gone, already missing him even though he'd only been out of the room a few minutes. He was in deep shit already and he knew it.

His mom shook her head. "Then I hope your faith in him is well founed and that he makes you happy. That's all I ever want for you." She squeezed both his hands. "And know that if things don't work out, I'll be here no matter what with plenty of ice cream and a shoulder to cry on." Brit already knew that, but it was good to hear.

A pounding on one of the doors interrupted what Brit wanted to say. He peered outside and rolled his eyes at the naked guy looking back at him through the gap in the curtains.

"Tell Logan to come on out. We'll show him a real good time." He shimmied his hips, and Brit let the curtain fall back into place.

"If that's the best he could do, I really doubt that," Mom commented flatly. "I want a man with some kind of rhythm. That boy is drunk off his ass."

"Security is on their way," Logan said as he returned to the room. "I'm sorry about this. Some people think that because I'm famous or because they might have met me that they have a right to try to come see me." He stayed away from the windows and actually seemed scared. Maybe he was right to be. Brit was mostly annoyed and wanted the naked trio gone.

He slipped his arm around Logan's waist. "Do you know any of those guys?"

Logan shook his head. "Not really. They may have been here once. Grant and his group might have brought them over a while ago. I'm not sure." He really seemed thrown. "This is supposed to be a controlled community, but Grant always has a lot of guys over at his place, and…."

"Why don't we get dinner started and let the security people handle Mr. Wiggle-hips and his friends? I'm sure they are more than capable of taking care of a few drunks."

"Good idea," Brit said gently, trying to let go of his worry about the kinds of things Logan might have done. "We can't let them ruin our night."

Logan leaned close. "Thank you," he whispered and kissed him, adding more than a touch of heat. Brit swore that if his mother wasn't there, he probably would have pushed Logan down onto the sofa and ridden him into next week. There was something about him that Brit couldn't figure out, but it drew him to Logan like a moth to flame. It was impossible to get enough. He wasn't sure Logan was good for him, but that didn't seem to matter.

"Are you two going to stand there playing kissy-face all evening?" Mom quipped.

Pulling away from Logan was the last thing Brit wanted to do, but he did, and the two of them got started with dinner.

SECURITY FOR the community arrived and got the naked crew out of the pool, dressed, and off the property. Brit and Logan made dinner while Mom sat at the counter. "Cynthia, what is it you do?"

"I was a surgical nurse for a lot of years. I've been thinking about retiring, but I don't really want to. Not yet. Now I work the floor in the ICU most of the time. It's a little less stressful, and as I get older, I like that. Because I have seniority, I work first shift, and I really love it. I help people get through some very tough health issues, and I love it when they leave the unit because they're getting better."

"Do you get to know your patients?" Logan asked.

Mom shrugged. "Sometimes. But if I'm really lucky, they aren't in the unit long enough for me to.

Our goal is to stabilize them and get them on the road to recovery so they don't have to stay with us any longer."

Logan opened the bottle of wine and poured them each a glass.

Mom wrapped her slender hands around the stem. "There are people who don't make it...." She took a sip and stayed silent for a few seconds.

"I suppose it happens," Logan said softly. "That can't be easy."

Mom shook her head. "But I suppose after a lot of years, you insulate yourself. I mean, I've seen people pass away on the operating table, and I've had them pass in the ICU. The good part of the job is seeing those who recover. The others... well, it is what it is, and we work hard to avoid it." She took another drink of her wine.

"This is turning out to be an interesting evening, from people breaking into the backyard and being flashed through the window to discussing people dying. What's next? Hey, can we talk about the big one and how we're all going to slide into the ocean?"

"I have a theory on that," Logan snarked.

Brit put his hands on his hips. "I just bet you do. But let's talk about something more interesting and less depressing." He got the whole-wheat pasta cooking and started warming the sauce. It was just something from a jar, but he had doctored it up to make it taste better. "We report on Monday to the studio." He was so excited. "This is going to be really cool."

"Will you be working closely together?" Mom asked.

"Some of the time. Brit and I have some scenes together, so they'll shoot them when we're both there. Other days he won't be needed, and there are times when they won't need either of us. There will be times, usually after principal shooting, that the cinematographer and the director will go out to get the ancillary shots. Like of the city or landscape." Brit let his mom and Logan talk, half listening while he finished making dinner. They talked movies and stuff for a while.

"What about your family?" Cynthia asked. "Your parents have to be proud of you."

"My folks are gone." Logan reached for a bottle and poured himself a large vodka. "My dad was killed in an accident. I was in the car with him, and...." He took a few swallows. "He died in front of me."

Mom held his hands. "I know that's tough. I see hurting families all the time. I'm no therapist—I talk way too danged much—but I know it helps to talk about it. And that stuff is only false courage. It won't take away that old pain."

Logan pushed his glass away. "But it sure makes it so you don't have to think about it."

"Maybe. But then when the booze wears off, you have to wonder what the hell bad things you did that you can't remember." His mom was good; Brit knew that for sure. "Did you get to say goodbye to him?"

Logan nodded. "I did. He and I got a few minutes where he was conscious and I got to tell him that I loved him. He told me the same...." More words just didn't come.

"Then know that you did all you could and that he wasn't alone in the end. That's all any of us can hope for. I know I sound like the queen of platitudes, but none of us gets to choose when we go, and the most we can hope for is that it will be quick and that there will be someone to hold our hand."

Brit kept quiet and finished dinner so it wasn't midnight before they were eating.

"Thank you, Cynthia," Logan said just as Brit put plates on the counter and set the food out so they could make up their plates.

"You're welcome." Her smile faded a little, and her expression grew serious.

"Mom, you aren't going to give Logan the 'if you hurt my son' speech, are you?" Brit asked.

She turned to him. "I was, as a matter of fact." She patted Logan's cheek. "I'm sure you can figure out what I was going to say." Dang, he hadn't seen that freeze-your-nuts-off look from his mother in years. "I will come after you if you hurt him."

Logan put his hands up. "I get the picture. I promise." He took a step back.

Brit loved his mother more than anything, and he knew she could be like a tiger, but there was nothing she could do if Brit ended up with a broken heart. Still, he wasn't going to let fear ruin what he might have with Logan. He knew that come good or bad, his heart had already chosen Logan, and there was little he could do about it. All he could do was hope that Logan felt the same way and was willing to treat his heart with the care that Brit would hold Logan's with if it were offered. One thing he knew for sure—only time would tell.

CHAPTER 5

THE FIRST day on set was always a little chaotic, and this one was no exception. "Are you sure you want to share your trailer?"

Whether on location or in the studio, Logan had his own trailer. It gave him some private space in an otherwise public world.

"I'm sure they can find a space for Brit for the few weeks he's here." Carlton pulled in a suitcase and started unpacking some of the things he'd brought to stock the fridge and the cupboards. "It seems like yesterday that we were in this trailer while you worked on *Knockout*."

Logan sprawled on the sofa in the front of the compact space. "I don't mind sharing." He hated the tension between Carlton and Brit. He got it from both of them, and he wished they could get along. "Besides, he and I have work to do together." Logan sighed as he sat up, legs spread out, already in the suit for his opening scene. There was always a sense of excitement and anticipation at the start of a project like this, and he tried not to let it overwhelm him, though what he really wanted was a damned drink. That would calm him down, even though it was still early.

"I know you get wired, and I have something for you if you need it." Carlton reached into his pocket as the trailer door opened and Brit climbed in.

"This is just so exciting. I've done lots of theater, and this reminds me of the best opening night ever," Brit enthused. He practically bounced over to Logan, kissed him hard, and wrapped his arms around his neck. "Don't you feel it?"

Logan nodded and closed his eyes, basking in Brit's energy.

"That will change after you work for eighteen hours, sleep for three hours, and then do it all over again," Carlton deadpanned. Logan knew what was coming. "Here," Carlton said, handing Logan a couple of pills. Logan took them and held them in his hand.

"What are those?" Brit asked Carlton.

"Just something to help him relax a little." Carlton handed Logan a bottle of water.

Brit leaned close. "You don't need those. We went over all the scenes we're shooting for the next two days, and you were awesome. That will only make you dull." Brit lightly kissed him behind the ear, sending a zip of energy through him. "Besides, you want to be in top form so that when we get a break, you and I can lock ourselves in the trailer and break in the bed back there properly."

Damn, Brit was incredible and made Logan forget about everything else, which was exactly what he was trying to do.

"I love that suit on you. It makes me think of James Bond… the really hot one."

A knock sounded. "Places in fifteen."

"Thank you." Brit moved away and turned to Carlton. "Does Logan have a prescription for those?"

Carlton's eyes went as big as saucers, and Logan took Brit's hand as he stood ramrod straight. He expected fire from Brit's eyes at any second. "Logan is an amazing actor, and yes, the days will be long and he's going to be as tired as hell, but that stuff isn't going to help him… or me." Brit turned to Logan, his eyes softer, almost pleading. "Please don't use that shit. Channel the energy and nerves into your performance. Remember, you're fucking Logan Steele and you can do anything." He was so damned sincere that Logan could almost believe him. "Please…."

How in the hell could he look into those huge eyes and not say yes? "Okay." Logan dropped the pills into the trash can.

"Seriously?" Carlton asked. "This is a hard business, and you know it."

Brit didn't move an inch. "I know he can do this. He's already worked hard, and there was none of that shit involved." Brit held his hand, watching Logan.

Logan knew this was one of those moments where he needed to be strong—not just for Brit, but for himself. "Take it away and don't bring it back." He stood and waited for Carlton to leave, then turned to Brit. "Are you going to come with me?"

"Yup." Brit grinned. "Just think, I get to see the great Logan Steele in action in front of the camera. I've already seen you in action in other places." He grinned again, and for a few seconds he looked like a teenager. Logan knew that Carlton was right and that things would get busy and wearing, but for now he'd let Brit be excited, and Logan would ride that energy for as long as he could.

LOGAN STRODE into the office setting for the eighth time, delivered his lines, and met the gaze of the man who was supposed to be his asshole boss. This scene was actually somewhere in the first third of the movie, and Logan knew he nailed it, especially as the lines rolled off his tongue as though they were *his* words, with his emotions behind them. The best part was that he could just see Brit at the edge of his vision, and it centered him in a way he hadn't been before.

"Cut!" Chris Halberton, the director, called. "That was the one I wanted," he added, and Logan sighed and stepped out of the set so they could set up for the next scene. This business was one of intense activity on his part, followed by heavy concentration, and then waiting around until he was needed again.

Brit stayed in the background, but Logan knew he was there. The first of his scenes would come that afternoon, and Logan was interested in watching. "Are you ready for me?" Logan asked.

"Yes. Just take it easy," Chris told him. "This is the part of the film where you are calm and collected. At this point, you haven't discovered how close to home things are going to become."

Logan looked out over the people assembled, and they all grew quiet as they took their positions. Logan was ready, and Chris called for action. He did the scene

exactly the way he and Brit had rehearsed it together
and how he had reviewed the character with Chris.

"That was great," Brit told him once the scene was
done and Logan had joined him. They had a longer
scene break while they prepared for the next shot—the
first one where Logan and Brit worked together.

"Are you ready? Did Chris talk to you about what
he wants?" Logan asked.

Brit shrugged. "It was kind of weird, but I don't
know if he understood what I was saying. He nodded
and seemed to listen but then didn't say too much." He
bit his lower lip. "I'm going to really go for it, and if he
doesn't like it, he can tell me and we'll do it again." He
seemed okay with that.

"If Chris didn't like it, he would have said so. I've
heard that he's the type of guy who has to see it." Logan
had never worked with Chris either, and he had an idea
that maybe this was going to take some feeling out for
everyone.

"I want to try something," Chris announced.
"There's the planned shot that connects these two we
just did. I want to run that one, but I want to do it with
all three at once, just one continuous scene, and let's
see what we get. So, everyone take your places and let's
see if we can get it in one or two takes."

Logan hadn't been expecting this, and he tensed.

"You'll be great, and I'm going to be just over
here," Brit told him. "Now go make a movie." He
smiled that same smile Logan had seen in the theater
that first night, and just like then, it sent his heart racing. Logan knew he was getting in pretty deep with
Brit, and he liked it, but it also worried him. Relation-
ships in the movie business didn't tend to last very long.
There were exceptions, of course, but the norm was like

everything else in Hollywood: they burned bright and hot and then faded. Logan had a routine, and he knew it. Most of the time when he brought a guy over, they had sex, and then he was gone in the morning. A few times, things had lasted longer, and then they were gone after a few days. Logan had been fine with that.

And to start with, that was what he'd expected to happen with Brit. But it hadn't. Brit had touched not just his body but his heart, and Brit saw him for more than just Logan Steele. Logan hadn't been prepared for that, and he still wasn't sure what it meant, other than the fact that he wanted to be the man that Brit deserved. He hoped he could.

WITH THAT entire scene done, Logan went back to his trailer while they set up for the next one. They most likely had an hour, and he wanted a few minutes of quiet. Brit followed him, practically bouncing off the walls in excitement. He spent a few minutes on the phone with his friend Clive, telling him how everything went. It was great hearing everything from Brit's perspective, even if he did his best not to listen in—something nearly impossible in the small space. Logan was glad Brit had a good friend. In this business, he was going to need it.

"I half expected Carlton to be here," Brit said once he hung up.

"He wanted to be on set, but the production crew offered me an assistant, and he has plenty to do already. There will be promotional tours, as well as a ton of things to stay on top of. Just because I'm filming doesn't mean the world out there comes to a halt." Logan eyed the bottles sitting on the counter next to the sink. Damn, that would sure as hell take the edge off. But he turned away. That kind of thinking was what had gotten him in trouble on the set of *Knockout*, and he knew damned well his career hung on the success of this picture. If he didn't come through, his career would be going downward faster than an out-of-control elevator. He had to do his best.

Of course, that meant he was constantly thinking about doing his best and being at his best, which only added to the stress. Then he was thinking about how he was getting stressed and that he needed to do something about it. Which only made him want a drink more. Then he worried that would dull his performance, and then he worried about the movie not being good enough and him not being good enough and the movie not doing well, which would start the downward elevator gaining speed, which added more stress, making him want a drink even more… and dammit. He held his head in his hands, wanting a drink so fucking bad he was shaking.

"Have you met him yet—the assistant?" Brit asked as a knock sounded, and then the door opened.

"You mean her. This is Margot," Logan added.

Brit hurried over to her and shook her hand. "I'm Brit. It's great to meet you." He smiled in that way he had that, even when it wasn't directed at him, made Logan happy inside because he knew Brit was happy.

"I wanted to check if you needed anything," Margot said.

Brit turned to Logan, and Logan shrugged, hanging on as best he could until this urge passed and his heart rate slowed back to normal. "Maybe a little lunch. Something light," Brit answered for him, "and something to drink without caffeine."

"Chicken salad and a diet soda along with whatever Brit wants," Logan said, and Margot was off a few seconds later. "I think I need something solid in my stomach, and no protein shakes. I'll fart the entire way through shooting, and they'll have to cut once the other actors keel over." At least Logan was finding a little of his sense of humor. He pulled Brit to him. "Stay away from that stuff. Did you see *Stranded*, one of my first movies, when I was trapped in the trunk of that damned car with Antonio what's-his-name? He kept drinking those damned shakes, and I nearly passed out from the gas. He and I joked about it the last time we saw each other. I still think of him as the exterminator. I swear they had to destroy the car after that. The smell permeated everything."

Brit chuckled. "Okay. No protein shakes."

They shared a soft laugh, and Logan felt more like himself. "Are you ready for your scene?"

"Yeah. I have all the lines down, and I know how I want to play it." Even he was a little nervous; Logan could feel it in the way his hand shook. "You going to be okay?"

"Oh yeah. I'm always this way before a performance. As soon as I get there, everything will fall away and I'll be ready to go." He was so confident. Logan wished he could bottle it so he could drink some of that.

Margot returned with lunch, and they ate and sat quietly. Logan ran through his next scene in his mind, and he and Brit went over things again. By the time the knock came, they were ready. Both of them brushed and flossed their teeth, then strode over to the set and got into position.

Working with Brit was unlike anything Logan had ever done before. He exuded energy, his movements big like he was playing to the back of the house. "Cut," Chris said after they got halfway through the scene. "Oh my God," he said through chuckles. "Okay, this is good, but you aren't on stage. Make your movements smaller and a little more intimate. It's just me and the camera. The audience will see what the camera does."

Brit seemed to take in every word. "I see."

"There isn't a back of the house," Chris instructed. "Think intimate, like letting people into your personal space."

"Got it," Brit said.

The next take was perfection, with energy, vitality, and Brit's own ray of sunshine that seemed to beam from inside him. When Chris ended the scene that time, he was silent afterward, and Logan turned to Brit, who shifted his weight from foot to foot.

"Perfect. Let's move on," Chris said, and Brit shared a grin with him before they went on to the next shot.

THE HOURS passed as the next camera shot just wasn't working no matter what any of them did. Chris was frustrated, as was everyone else. It happened, and sometimes you just kept working until you got the shot, even if the director didn't know what the shot was until it happened. Finally Chris wrapped shooting for the day at nearly midnight.

Brit followed Logan back to the trailer. "Should we go home?"

Logan shook his head. "Just clean up and climb into bed. We need to be in makeup and wardrobe in five hours." He drank some water and used the bathroom before climbing into the bed next to Brit. He was exhausted, and yet his mind refused to close down.

Brit rolled onto his side and ran his hand down Logan's arm. "Just relax and stop worrying. You looked great today, and Chris was happy. I know there's a long way to go, but all you need to do is take it one thing at a time instead of worrying about everything all at once. Close your eyes and rest. We have another long day tomorrow."

EVERY DAY seemed long, with no rest in sight. A week of the grueling schedule wore on everyone... except Brit. He always seemed so bright and cheerful. Logan had thought about picking a fight just to see him ruffled, but he was already tired, and there were many weeks of principal shooting left to go. He'd only been able to spend a single night in his own bed, and even then he hadn't slept much. Still, he was making it through.

Logan arrived on set on time and ready to go. Brit was already there. He showed up all the time, not wanting to miss anything. "We have an issue with one of the cameras," Chris told Logan when he wondered why everyone was standing around. He'd found that Chris was efficient and kept things moving if at all possible. "It will be a couple of hours."

"Okay," Logan said.

Brit joined him. "Let's go to the trailer. We can lie down for a while and get a little nap before you're needed."

He and Brit headed across the lot to the trailer, but when he opened the door, he found Carlton sitting at the table.

"I thought we could go over some things. I heard there's a delay." He seemed so chipper Logan wanted to smack him.

"Is it urgent?" Logan asked.

"No, but it will be," Carlton said.

Logan plopped himself in the seat across from him. He barely listened as Carlton went over some promotional ideas, and all Logan could do was shake his head. "The movie isn't near done. I suggest you put together a detailed plan, and then once that's ready, we can go over it." He was putting Carlton off by giving him work to do. "Also, go to the house and make sure everything is okay. If Grant shows up, send him and his pool buddies away. Even if I get a night off, I'm going to need to rest." He stood. "Please let yourself out." He was too tired to be nice at this point, and he wanted to down half the bottle of vodka. Then he'd be out of it and he could sleep for hours.

Brit guided him back and closed the partition to the rest of the trailer. The window curtains were closed, and as much light had been blocked out as possible.

"Just rest, and I'll make sure someone wakes you in plenty of time." Brit kissed him gently.

"Please stay," Logan asked, and Brit lay down next to him.

Logan closed his eyes, put an arm around Brit, and just let go of everything. These two hours were precious for multiple reasons, not least of which was because Brit was right there with him. He wasn't alone, and Logan was coming to understand that he could do anything as long as Brit was there.

CHAPTER 6

"YOU WANTED to see me?" Brit asked outside one of the mobile offices.

"Yes, come in," a middle-aged man said and motioned to a chair. "I know this is a little unorthodox, but we've been watching the daily rushes, and your work has been amazing."

Brit nodded. "Thank you."

"I'm sorry. I'm getting ahead of myself. James Carlysle. I'm one of the producers of this picture, and we've really been impressed. I know you were contracted for three weeks' work, but there are some rewrites taking place, and we're consolidating a few smaller parts into yours. It will streamline the story a little."

Brit swallowed. "You want to make my part bigger?" This was great news.

"Yes. There were a few small parts in the film that are being rewritten slightly, and their function in the story will be handled by your character instead. As I said, your work has been really great, and all of us have come to like a character that in the beginning was just a throwaway."

"Thank you… I think," Brit said.

"No." He stood and shook Brit's hand. "Thank you. It was your work that brought Ambrose to life and made him someone we all really love. You'll be on set for a few more weeks toward the end of shooting. I'll have my people contact your agent to work out the details."

"That's great."

James settled back in his chair. "I have even better news. My partners are working on a film with Universal. We showed them your rushes, and they have a part for you. It's small, just a few weeks' work, but it should work around your schedule here. Again, we'll send all the details to your agent. But we're all real glad to be working with you." He stood, and Brit got up and headed for the door. "It's always a pleasure to see real talent bloom right in front of your eyes." James smiled, and Brit left the small office area and went back out in the heat. He stood outside as sets and racks of costumes passed by like he was on a movie preparation superhighway.

"Oh my God," Brit said. He pulled out his phone and immediately messaged his agent, as well as his mother. They were making his part bigger, and they had another one for him. This was beyond his wildest imagination. Once he sent the messages, he hurried back to the trailer to try to find Logan.

He was on the set, and Brit stayed off to the side until the shot was done. Logan looked amazing. He was tired—they both were—but the circles under his eyes had dissipated and his eyes were bright, like maybe he had gotten all that crap Carlton had been foisting on him out of his system. When Chris cut the take and told the team to set up the next one, Brit waited for Logan to come over.

"What did the producers want? Is there some sort of problem?"

Brit shook his head. "Apparently they love my work. They're doing some rewrites and are going to make my part bigger. And their production company has a project at Universal, and they have a part in it for me." He could barely keep himself from shaking apart. "It looks like I'm here another week and will work over there for a few weeks before returning here for some final shooting in a month or so." He was going to be really busy, but good things were happening.

Logan hugged him right there, his strong arms enclosing him. "That is so wonderful. I knew you were that good and that all someone had to do was see you." He lifted Brit off the ground and twirled him around before setting him back on his feet. "I'm so happy for you."

"Me too." He rested his head against Logan's chest.

"What is it?" Logan asked.

"Who is going to look after you?" Brit asked, knowing it was likely a difficult topic.

Logan narrowed his eyes in his classic scowl. "You mean watch over me to make sure I'm good?"

Brit lightly smacked his shoulder. "No. I mean, who is going to make sure you eat well and get some rest instead of using every spare minute to be inundated with details that aren't important?" He practically growled as Carlton stood off to the side, probably waiting to ask Logan some stupid question that he didn't need to deal with right now. "Who will put you first before their petty jealousies and whatever they want from you?" A person could only take so much. "I just want you to be able to concentrate on your work." He didn't mention Carlton by name because it was a touchy subject, but he always seemed to be hanging around, even though he wasn't really needed. Margot did a better job than he did anyway. Maybe Brit could talk to her and make sure she watched over Logan a little.

"I'll be fine. I can take care of myself," Logan told him.

"I know you can. But you rarely tell anyone no, even when they're being a pain in the butt." Logan was just too damned nice sometimes. "I'll worry about you."

"Logan, I have some papers and things for you to look over," Carlton said.

Brit bit his lower lip. "Did his lawyer see them? Or his agent? That's what he has them for." He was getting snippy, but he saw Carlton as a hanger-on rather than someone who added real value.

"He usually handles these himself," Carlton countered.

Logan took what Carlton had in his hand, looked them over, and then told Carlton to forward them to his agent. Brit tried not to look smug. Thankfully he was an actor. "I think they're almost ready for you on set," Brit said before stepping away and moving to the back so he could watch. Logan went to the makeup chair, where an artist touched up his face with a little powder so his skin didn't shine.

"You know, Logan is going to move on soon enough. He always does," Carlton said quietly from next to him.

Brit shrugged and didn't turn toward Carlton in the slightest. "Maybe he will." He didn't want to contemplate how right Carlton could turn out to be. "And maybe he won't. But Logan isn't in love with you, and he never will be. He doesn't see you that way, and as much as you might like him to be, that will never happen."

Carlton's sharp intake of air told Brit he had hit the nail on the head. Granted, it hadn't been a huge leap. Brit had seen the way Carlton looked at Logan when he thought no one saw him, like a lovesick teenager high on their first hit of hormones.

Carlton stood stock-still. "My so-called feelings for him aren't what's important."

"Sure they are. You're supposed to be his manager, and falling for your boss isn't the most professional thing to do, and you know it. You're supposed to be helping him, looking after his career and his schedule, making sure he's taken care of, and instead…." Brit left that hanging and shook his head as everyone got into position. He remained silent, watching Logan as he got ready for the shot. Everyone grew quiet, and Brit crossed his arms over his chest, doing his best to pretend Carlton wasn't there. Instead, he concentrated on Logan, sending him all the good vibes he could.

They ran through the scene four times, and then Chris said he had enough and the crew set up for the next take.

"I've been with Logan for five years," Carlton said.

"I know." Brit wanted to be snarky, but the words died on his lips. "And I'm a guy he met six weeks ago, and now I'm on set and have parts in movies because of him."

"And you'll just use him and that will be that," Carlton said softly.

"I don't know what will happen. But I can tell you this—Logan is wonderful, and I see him for the person he is. And I *like* him for who he is." He bit his lower lip before returning his attention to Logan and the scene they were still setting up. "How many people can you honestly say fall into that category? Do you?" Brit asked.

"I do my very best for him, and I always have. This is a tough business, and it takes a lot out of people. Long hours, pressure, tension, expectations that are way too much for anyone to handle on their own." So far Carlton hadn't said anything that Brit didn't know and hadn't already seen.

"What's your point? Better living through chemistry? Getting him up with one pill and then down with another? That isn't helping." Brit kept his voice soft enough that only Carlton could hear him.

Carlton grew defensive, his entire body tensing, but Brit had had enough of this conversation. He shifted positions to leave Carlton alone.

"What do you know about anything?" Carlton asked as he came up behind him. "So he's needed some help from time to time. That doesn't make him a bad person."

Brit whirled around. "I never said it did. But you know that stuff can take over. It's happened time and time again. And you've seen the work he's been doing. He's been amazing these past few weeks, and his confidence is growing. All that the drink and the pills do is take that away from him. They're crutches that are too easy to rely on." He sure as hell wasn't going to go into the effects that substance abuse had had on his family, but he had seen it firsthand, and Brit didn't want Logan to go through that. Maybe this was exactly what his mother had been trying to warn him about.

"There are times when he needs some help," Carlton whispered.

Brit glared. "I'm not saying you shouldn't help him." He wasn't going to get through to Carlton, because in his mind, Carlton thought he was helping Logan. That idea hit Brit hard. Granted, Brit thought he was helping Logan too, and he hoped that was true. Logan seemed to be performing well. His eyes were bright and he had energy, sometimes maybe a little too much, but that was better than him being drugged and out of it. What was coming through now was the real Logan Steele, not some drugged-down version.

Brit caught Logan's eyes, and they shared a smile. Then he motioned toward the door, and Logan hurried over. "You okay?"

"Yeah. I'm just going back to the trailer for a little bit. I want to make a few calls. But I'll be back after a little while." He smiled and was tempted to stay right where he was, basking in the light from Logan's eyes. "I shouldn't be too long."

Logan nodded. "Okay. I'll see you later."

"Margot is right over there," Brit told him, trying to take some of the emphasis off Carlton. That guy was really too embroiled in Logan's business, but there was nothing he could do about it. Getting involved in that relationship was a battle that would come eventually, but one he wasn't equipped to fight now.

"I have this last shot and then I'll have a break for a while," Logan told him. "I'll just come to the trailer."

"Great. We can go over our scenes and make sure we have everything down," Brit offered and hurried away before he became tempted to stay and watch Logan. He left the sound stage and pulled out his phone.

"I thought you had dropped off the face of the earth," Clive said when he answered the call. "So how are things in the big bad world of movies? Are you a movie star yet? Can I tell friends I knew you when...?"

"Stop it." Brit reached the trailer and went inside, closed the door, and let the air-conditioned atmosphere cool off his skin. "I am on my way, I hope. I have another part. The producers love my work and offered me a part in another of their movies. It's not huge and I haven't seen the script, but it's good, and I'm working here and not doing those damned voice-overs."

"So you quit?"

"I was a contractor, so I'm just not taking any jobs right now, and I hope I never will again." God, this was almost as good as having Logan in his life, but not quite. That was the brightest spot.

"Then why the tinge of worry in your voice?" Clive could always read him so well. "Things are going well with work, you have the sexiest boyfriend on earth, which has everyone jealous, and you seem so happy. Is there trouble in paradise?"

"Logan's manager," Brit said.

"Oh. His pusher and enabler?" He and Clive had talked before. "Did you have it out with him like I said?"

"No. I did talk to him, and I can't quite read him. I want to think he's a bad guy, but maybe not. I'm not a fan of the man, and I think he's encouraging Logan to take the easy way out sometimes. But it isn't all Carlton's fault. He isn't pouring the alcohol down Logan's throat or forcing him to take the pills and shit."

"No, he just supplies them," Clive said. "And he makes that behavior easy." He paused, and Brit waited for his friend. His inclination was to keep talking, so a pause from Clive was meaningful. "Honey, you may not want to hear what I have to say." Brit swallowed. "But… Logan needs to make his own decisions. Carlton can't do that for him, and neither can you, no matter how much you might want to and think you have his best interests at heart."

"I know…." Brit sighed. "I can see what all that stuff was doing to him. You should see him now. He's intense and luminous. It's amazing to see." He was so excited. "And he has so much energy." He giggled like a schoolkid. "Yesterday while we were on a two-hour break… well, let's just say that we're all lucky those stages are soundproof, because we would have interrupted a number of projects in progress." Brit snickered.

"Did you scare the straight people?' Clive asked.

"We really weren't *that* loud, but I was really happy that trailer has good suspension." He sat down on one of the banquette seats. "The point is that I really think Logan is coming into himself once again."

Clive hesitated for a few seconds. "Then that's all you can do. There comes a point where you can show Logan that things are possible, and from there he has to make his decisions for himself. I just hope he makes the right ones."

Deep down Brit knew Clive was right. Logan had promised him that he would try to stay away from the pills and alcohol, but Brit knew that was a pie-crust promise, easily made and easily broken, especially when the pressure piled up and everyone wanted something from him. As much as Brit wanted to blame Carlton for things, Logan was responsible for his own actions and decisions. "Me too." Brit swallowed hard. The thought of Logan at the mercy of some of the people in his life scared the hell out of him. "I just wish I could help him not be so alone all the time. His friends…." He sighed.

"The bikini boys you told me about?" Clive asked.

"They're all there for a good time, and not one of them gives a crap about Logan other than what he can do for them." Brit didn't like the way they behaved at all.

"Yes, I get that. But do you not like them because of that, or because of the fact that you're worried they will show up when you're not there and that Logan will decide to partake of what they're offering?" Sometimes Clive's aim was just too damned good. "Because you're going to need to learn to trust Logan. I know that's hard for you, with your dad and everything. But that's something you're going to need to work on. Jealousy isn't called the green-eyed *monster* for nothing."

Brit sighed. He hated it when Clive was right. It rankled him, especially since trusting wasn't his strong suit. Oh, Brit liked to think he was strong and confident and that he could take whatever he had to, but he was realizing that Logan held a place in his heart that no one else had, and that made him vulnerable. Brit hated being open to someone that way. "I know, but you should see that shit. The last time there were, like, seven guys, and all of them were these gorgeous *GQ* model types with their shirts open and abs that look like they had been cut with chisels." Maybe he was whining a little.

"And what are you, chopped liver? Logan chose you, and he pursued you and actually asked someone to come see our performance and got you noticed. I'd say you need to give the guy a break and back off. He has to sink or swim. You can't do it for him." Clive seemed to grow more animated.

"I know that," Brit tried to counter, but the words fell flat because that *was* what he'd been trying to do.

"You're in love with the guy and he has some issues, so you try to take all that away from him so he can be a better person. Does that sound familiar? Remember Claude three years ago? The guy was a mess, but he was cute and sort of gangly and naïve, but man, did he have problems. You liked the guy when all of us told you he was beyond help."

Brit growled in his throat. "You promised you'd never bring that up again."

"Maybe you need reminding. You fell for the guy and woke up one morning to your wallet, television, camera, and anything else that he could lay his hands on gone. I'm surprised he didn't take the sheets and leave your ass literally dangling in the wind. He sold everything to get a hit of whatever he was on."

Brit shivered. "That's pretty low. And it wasn't that bad." He groaned to himself because at the time it had been pretty terrible. "At least I found where he dumped my wallet and ID and I was able to stop all my cards and stuff."

"That's not the point. You had this soft spot for Claude, and I can't help wondering if Logan is the same thing all over again." Leave it to Clive to be the voice of reason.

"And you've had better luck?" Brit countered.

"Nope. My past losers could form a parade that would stretch down Colorado Boulevard farther than the Rose Parade. But that's not the issue. I know I'm a loser magnet, and I'm dealing with that by giving up men and becoming a hermit with just my computer and internet porn for company. Oh, and by the way, I have all of your work bookmarked so I can hear your voice any time I want, even when you're too busy to call." Clive cackled at that, and Brit rolled his eyes. "Say, to change the subject, do the people you're working with know about your past boom-chicka-mow-mow work?"

Bit shook his head. "I don't think so, though I haven't kept it a particular secret. Not that it's really important. I never did anything under my real name, and the voice work was uncredited. There isn't a way to trace me directly to what I did."

Clive clicked his teeth. "This is Hollywood. There is always a way for someone to find out. You got paid by the production company, and it wouldn't be hard for someone to trace that. And if they do, they could conclude that you were on the receiving end of a little on-camera spit-roast or something." He was having way too much fun with this.

"I suppose. But who do I tell? I'm not some big star. I have one small part in a movie. Few people are going to be paying attention to me, really." He settled back on the seat. "I think I have to go. I promised Logan that I wouldn't be gone long, and I've learned so much just from watching what people do. It's really fascinating, like this whole little city coming together for a short time to make this movie. Everyone has their job and they all know what they're doing, and they work together really well even though they may not have met each other before." He got up and grabbed a bottle of water from the refrigerator.

"Nice change of subject. But to get back to my point, you need to tell your agent so they know and can help you manage the situation should it come up. As for Logan… sweetheart, you have to do what you think is best. You know I love you more than my luggage and that I'll always be here, but I would prefer not to have to come help you put your heart back together again. I like it when you're happy."

"I know that, and right now I am." Brit was going to have to see how things worked out. He didn't have a crystal ball.

"Then go out there and find Mr. Wonderful. Be happy and knock 'em dead. You always did with the theater, so I know you'll be amazing." Brit could always count on Clive to be supportive. "I love you, sweetheart, and if that man doesn't treat you right, I promise I'll come down there and put Bengay in all his underwear." He signed off, and Brit slipped his phone into his pocket, chuckling as he grabbed his water and left the trailer to head back to the sound stage. It was closed, with a guard blocking entrance.

"Sorry, Brit, they're shooting."

He leaned against the side of the building and drank his water. "No problem. I can wait."

"How is it going?" the guard asked.

Brit tried to remember if he'd been introduced, but couldn't remember his name. There were quite a few people around, and it was hard to remember everyone, but he tried his best. "Pretty good. This is my first part in a movie, and I'm real excited about it."

The guard leaned closer. "You're killing it. People talk in front of us all the time, and they don't think we can hear them. Everyone is talking about how amazing you've been. I heard Chris telling someone that he would work with you any time and loves how you're always so prepared and on top of things."

"I'm glad to know that," Brit said with a smile. "I was hoping to make a good impression and to do my best." The guard's phone dinged, and he checked the message before opening the door. "Go on in."

Brit walked into the middle of a standoff between Logan and one of the other actors. Both stood toe-to-toe, glaring at each other. Brit wanted to jump in to come to Logan's defense, but that was a bad idea. He did step into Logan's field of vision, and almost immediately some of the tension drained out of him. Logan's stance relaxed and he lowered his arms. "You can't play it like that. It doesn't work or fit with the character." Logan shifted his weight and turned to Chris, who nodded.

"You have to play the character the way it's written, Harris. The improvising is throwing everyone off," Chris scolded. Brit never wanted to be on the receiving end of that particular cold expression.

Harris Towers was someone Brit had seen on television a number of times, and he had been brought into the movie to help add to star power. He'd only been on set a few days, and he'd been a disruption since the very first. It seemed Harris liked everything a certain way, and on his TV series, *Threesome*, he seemed to get whatever he wanted, but this was a different world.

"I'm making this awful script better," he countered. "If the writers had any talent at all, they would be able to make this dialogue—"

"That's enough," Chris interjected. "This isn't some ridiculous romantic comedy. It's an action picture, so stop acting like a buffoon and learn your character." For the first time since shooting began, frustration colored Chris's voice. "Let's clear the set for another take. Logan, give me a little more intensity, and Harris, a little less Lucille Ball." He got into position, and Brit waited while Logan and Harris did their scene again. This time Harris was awful, and Brit cringed as Chris cut the take. He spoke with Harris privately, and Brit could see the tension rising between them. Logan stood next to him, saying nothing but radiating stress.

"You got this," Brit said quietly. "You looked great."

"I want to smack the hell out of Harris. I've seen scene stealing and plenty of overacting, but this guy is just a hack. He has one arrow in his quiver, and we're expected to make a movie with that."

Brit lightly touched Logan's hand. He didn't want to be too publicly affectionate, but he wanted to show support.

"You can't control what he does, only yourself," Brit told Logan and then leaned close. "And right now I wish we were back at your house and we had the pool all to ourselves…." He winked, and Logan's eyes grew darker as he watched. Damn, Brit loved that he could do that to one of the sexiest men alive.

"Jesus," Logan breathed. "You're terrible." He groaned softly. "I'm going to have to think unsexy thoughts so I can get through this scene."

"As long as you know that I'm going to be watching you, getting more and more excited by the second." There was something about seeing Logan work with increased intensity each day. He really seemed to be throwing himself into his work, and it was sexy as hell. "I think you're needed now." He took a single step back, and Logan strode back on set.

Harris joined him, and everyone got into place. Chris got everyone quiet and called for action. Logan did the scene with all the almost frantic energy required of the character, with Harris delivering his lines but seeming to shrivel under Logan's presence. "Cut. Perfect," Chris called. "Let's move on."

"But I looked terrible," Harris complained, though it fell on deaf ears. Chris already had the team setting up the next shot.

"Then you'll need to do better and get your act together. Otherwise you will look the fool in a movie that isn't a comedy." Chris's expression was dead serious.

"This next shot is important and long, so let's get it in one." He directed the setup, and Logan joined Brit. Afterward they headed back to the trailer.

"Did your call go well?" Logan asked.

"Yes. I got a message while you were filming. Apparently tomorrow is a huge day. They plan to finish up with me for the time being, and then I'm needed at Universal. I'll be there for two or three weeks, and according to Chris's schedule, I'll be back here in five weeks for some of the location work." He opened the door and they stepped inside, where Margot was checking the refrigerator and the cupboards, making a list of what was needed.

"Do you think you could arrange for a nice dinner to be delivered?" Logan asked her. "He and I can eat it here. I have a feeling this is going to be another long one, and I'm tired of all this quick food."

"Of course. What would you like?" She grabbed a pad.

"I don't know. Maybe something light. Japanese would be great, but not sushi." Logan settled in the chair and stretched out his legs, yawning, his eyes half-lidded. They maybe had half an hour.

A knock sounded, and then the door opened. "Brit, they need you in wardrobe. Apparently they have changed their minds and you need to get dressed," one of the runners explained before taking off again. Brit took Logan's hand, and they shared a silent moment of camaraderie before Brit left to get himself to the set.

"THANK GOD we're nearly done for the day," Logan said softly. Brit had been sweating bullets in his heavy costume for hours.

"I hear that. I'm going to change out of this and turn it in so they can clean it." He hoped he never had to wear the heavy wool suit again. The air-conditioning in the studio had been struggling to keep up on a really hot day, and Brit felt like he was going to melt into a puddle. He left Logan and made his way over to wardrobe, where Bernice helped him out of the clothes that were sticking to his skin. "Sorry about this."

"No worries. We'll have it cleaned overnight," one of the wardrobe assistants told him. She handed him a towel, and he dried off before putting on his regular clothes. What Brit really needed was dinner, a shower, and then a chance to sleep in a bed that wasn't crammed into the back of a trailer. Not that there was anything wrong with the bed itself, but the studio tended to run twenty-four hours a day, which meant there could be noise outside at almost any time.

"You look worn out," Carlton was saying when Brit returned from changing. He let him and Logan talk and went to the bathroom to freshen up a little before joining them. "You really need to try to get some rest. There are months of shooting yet to go."

"I'm aware of that. Chris is setting a pretty demanding schedule right now, and we all need to keep up. The big special effects shots will be later in the schedule, and that will slow things down for the actors, but right now we all need to be on our game." Logan had only settled in his chair when there was a knock, followed by Margot coming in with dinner.

"Thank you," Brit said as Logan passed her some bills.

"Is that enough?" he asked her.

"I can get you change," she said gently.

"Not necessary. Just use it to get supplies later." Logan sat at the table. Brit was about to take the place across from him when Carlton slipped in. Brit sighed and shook his head. Sometimes Carlton could be completely dense.

"We have quite a few things to go over, and I thought we could review lines and things." Carlton pulled out a container and opened it. "I'm sure Brit has his own work to do."

Brit rolled his eyes, reached for the table, and lifted his container of food away from Carlton. It seemed the guy didn't do subtle. He stood at the counter near the sink and set the container aside.

Logan said, "Brit and I had planned a nice dinner, and then we have one more scene before we go home. After that we're going to sleep and will be back tomorrow. As you said, I'm worn out. We can run lines first thing in the morning so it's fresh. I'm set already for this next scene."

Carlton tensed as he got up. "Okay. I get the point."

"Thank you. I have a list of things that I need you to look at. I'll email them to you as soon as I'm done eating." Logan sat back, and Brit excused himself for a few seconds to let them talk until he heard the door close.

"I don't know what's up with him."

Brit certainly did, but he had tried to broach the subject before and Logan didn't seem to believe him, so he stayed quiet and settled at the table. He got out plates and put his food on one, then placed it in the microwave for thirty seconds. He did the same for Logan's before setting their plates on the table and getting them each something to drink.

"I think you deserve a beer if you want one," Brit said.

Logan shook his head, and Brit slid into his seat. "One of the producers came by while you were shooting your scene and remarked that they were pleased with my performance and that they had been worried because of the stories that surrounded *Knockout*. Apparently they have been keeping a closer eye on me than I thought." He took a bite. "They said they were pleasantly surprised." Logan sat back and set down his fork. "I didn't know I had become such a fuckup." He sighed. "You know, I grew up a good kid. I was the one who worked hard and always did his homework. I used to worry about it until I got it done."

Brit set down his fork and took Logan's hand. "Maybe that's the issue. Back then you had ways of dealing with the stress. You made sure to get your work done and then you didn't worry about it anymore. But what's happening now is a different kind of tension because you can't control it." He lightly squeezed Logan's fingers. "Producers, directors, other actors, the public—all of them have expectations, and you have no control over any of it."

"I guess." He picked up his fork once more. "And Harris isn't helping. That guy thinks he knows everything and how it should all be done, but he has no clue about anything. He's a one-trick pony, and other than that, there's very little there." He went back to eating. "What bothers me is that his performance is going to affect the movie."

Brit nodded. "Then all you can do is prop the guy up. Help him and bring him along so he doesn't tank all of us." He grinned. "Though maybe they'll just cut his part out if he's that bad."

Logan shook his head. "They're paying too much for the guy to do that, and they want his name up on the marquee to bring in people. It's all about the money and who you can get to go to the theater." Logan's hand began shaking. "I just want this damned thing to be stellar and a success. I'm giving it all I have." He closed his eyes. "And I want a drink so damned bad sometimes I can barely stand it. Today I was torn between punching Harris or screaming at everyone on set. I was barely holding it together."

"I didn't see that at all. You looked great, and when your character was supposed to be tense, you just went for it, and the anxiety was palpable. Maybe that's the key—just channel the crap with Harris into your performance." Brit wanted to help, and he hoped that his support was doing Logan some good.

"I can try," Logan said softly.

Brit tapped the table. "Go ahead and eat your dinner so we can brush and floss and get back out there in time." Logan ate a few bites, and Brit did the same. Once they were done, he put the leftovers in the refrigerator, and after they had cleaned up, they went back on set.

"YOU NEED to pay attention to what you're doing," Logan snapped at Harris. "You aren't in a screwball comedy. You're going to be hanging from the top of a building next and messing your pants, scared for your life. Cracking jokes and acting like an idiot is not going to cut it." He stormed off the set and out toward the door.

Brit was about to go after him, but Chris stopped him. "Brit, I think we're going to add you to the next shot. There won't be any lines, but I want your character to see this so we can use it later. You'll need to get to wardrobe right away. Margot, check on Logan."

Brit hurried out. He really wanted to see to Logan, but apparently he had gone in the opposite direction from the wardrobe area.

Brit got into costume and returned to the set, expecting to find Logan. Harris stood off to the side in tense conversation with Chris. Margot came in with Logan, whose eyes looked wild, his body so filled with tension he almost stomped rather than walked. Logan's eyes blazed with anger, and his hands were clenched into fists.

"Let's do one more take, and then we can move on and be done for the day." Chris got everyone into position. Brit watched as Logan transformed into his character, the tension easing out of him. Fucking hell, he was truly amazing to watch.

"Damn," Margot breathed from next to him just before Chris called for silence and then action. This time the shot went better, and once Chris called to cut, he seemed to have what he needed. Logan once again transformed, shooting Harris a murderous glare before stomping off the set. "Hell, I thought the storm was over."

Brit shook his head. "Nope. It just took a break. I think this is one battle that is going to go on for the entire length of shooting." It sure looked to Brit like this was a relationship that was doomed from the start. He checked the time and stifled a yawn as they got set up and ready. Brit got his instructions from Chris and took his place off to the side. All he had to do was walk in and sit down near where Logan and Harris were talking. A server would pass with a tray, and he was to take a glass and sip from it. He was just background dressing for this shot, and everything went fine once Logan returned until Brit sipped the drink and just about gagged. Still, he managed to hold it together and keep in character until the scene was over. "What the hell is this?" Brit asked, spitting and coughing as soon as the cameras stopped rolling.

Harris broke out laughing. "What did you do?" Logan demanded.

"Keep your panties on. I added lemon juice. It's a joke. I thought it would be funny." He continued laughing as Brit set down the glass, shaking his head.

"Let's run that again," Chris announced, and Brit glared as the glasses were switched out.

This time the scene went flawlessly until Harris was supposed to storm out of the room at the end of the scene. Brit extended his leg, and Harris stumbled over his foot and nearly fell flat on his face. Brit hadn't tripped him on purpose, but Harris turned on him, fuming.

"It was a joke," Logan quipped. "I thought it was funny." He puffed out his chest. "You can dish it out, but you can't take it."

"Okay, all of you settle down. Brit, that looked incredibly natural. We're going to keep that. I have an idea that may tie into. Now let's do the scene without any more jokes so we can all go home." They got into position once again, and this time the scene went the way Chris wanted.

Brit was so ready to leave and get a good night's sleep. After they returned from wardrobe, Logan called for a car, and they walked out to meet it at the private lot. A crowd of people stood outside the gate, and Logan waved while a few folks took pictures. Brit stayed in the background and let Logan have his time with his fans, getting into the car to wait for him. People shouted questions at him, but Logan just smiled and waved before climbing into the car as well and closing the door.

"I've forgotten what a gauntlet this can be," Logan said. "When we're huddled in our area on set, we're pretty insulated." He signaled to the driver that they were ready, and the car glided out of the studio, past the small group of people hoping to catch a glimpse of someone like Logan.

Brit leaned against him, closing his eyes. "I have to rest and then prepare for my scenes tomorrow." He yawned and sighed, fatigue washing over him.

"You should sleep," Logan whispered.

Brit knew he was right, but this was his chance, and he had to be prepared. "I'll be okay. It's just two scenes, and I can read them over and go through my lines before I go to bed." God, he hoped he didn't fall asleep right here.

In fact, he dozed off while they rode, and woke as the car pulled into Logan's drive. Brit got out and thanked the driver. He went inside, flopped down on the sofa, and picked up his script for tomorrow. His eyelids felt heavy, but he was determined to make the most of the opportunities coming his way.

"You need to come to bed," Logan said, and Brit realized he had dozed off, his script resting on his lap, his phone next to him from where he'd called Clive to talk for a few minutes. All this was becoming a little overwhelming, and he needed someone objective to help ground him.

"I know." He picked up the pages and forced his mind to function. "Just a little more."

Logan flopped onto the sofa next to him and snagged the script from his hands. "Let's run it and see where you are." He got to the start of the scene and started reading.

Brit knew the lines, but he hadn't quite figured out the character and how to play it.

"Less energy than what you're doing now. This character thinks more, so his humor is drier and more cerebral. After you land the line, wait for the others to catch up. Maybe just a second before going on. It will signal that he knows how smart he is, but doesn't want to rub it in," Logan explained.

"I've thought of that, but it doesn't quite seem right. Maybe pausing before delivering the line, like he knows it's funny and wants to make them wait for it." Brit got a tingle, energy flooding him as his fatigue faded. Logan ran the scene again, and this time it sang and felt perfect. Brit sighed and stood, holding out his hand.

"Time for bed?" Logan asked.

Brit wound his arms around his neck. "You and I have this whole house to ourselves. No small trailer and no guests. So, you go make sure everything is locked up, and then follow me." Brit slipped away and turned toward the glass doors overlooking the pool. He tugged off his shirt and let it flutter to the floor. Then he toed off his shoes and slipped off his pants, letting the last of his clothes slide down his legs. Once he'd stepped out of them, Brit opened the door and went outside, slowly walking to the pool before diving in.

He felt rather than heard Logan join him. Then he came up behind him, wet skin sliding against him, strong arms winding around his waist. "I've missed this."

"What? Sex in the pool?" Brit teased.

"No. Well, yes, but I missed having time with you like this. The quiet out here. I mean, we got a few hours here and there to be alone, but the trailer isn't this." He motioned to the city lights spreading out below them. "You can see all of that and you know it's loud and busy, yet up here, it's quiet ribbons of light with the mountains in back. All of it just for us."

Logan kissed him, pressing Brit back against the side of the pool. The cool water felt amazing against his hot skin. Logan lifted him out and onto the side of the pool, laying him down onto the coated concrete, sliding his lips down over his length, taking Brit one step closer to heaven.

He stared up at the sky, the few stars bright enough to be seen drawing closer as Logan played his body like a virtuoso. Brit gasped, running his fingers through Logan's soft, thick hair. "I don't want to go away," he whispered.

Logan hummed and took him deeper, as if echoing his sentiment using his lips in a very different way. Brit drew his legs upward, exposing himself to Logan, who took the opportunity to add more sensation, teasing Brit with the tips of his fingers on ultra-sensitive skin, sending shivers of desire through him. "What am I going to do without you?" He met Logan's gaze, cupping his cheeks in his hands. "Are you going to think me stupid if I say that we've spent the last few weeks together almost all of the time and I'm going to miss this?" He kissed him hard.

"Me too," Logan whispered. "Very few people seem to fit into my life without a ton of work. And I don't mean that in a lazy or bad way. You seem to understand me, and we fit." Logan kissed him again, running his hands down Brit's outer thighs. "And it isn't like I don't have to work with you—I do. But you make me better and want to be more, and I want the same for you."

Brit held Logan's cheeks. "I want the same for you too. But I keep wondering if…." He sighed. "If you wouldn't be happier with someone… I don't know, prettier or handsomer."

Logan chuckled and then began to laugh, pressing down on top of him. "You don't see yourself very well. Half the crew on that set watches you like you're dipped in whipped cream and they can't wait to lick you up and down. I have to keep my jealousy in check all the damned time, and it takes some effort to keep from growling at people when they look at you." He swallowed and held Brit in a gaze that had enthralled millions of people. "My mom used to say that beauty is only skin-deep, but with you, it goes much farther than that." Logan's gaze intensified as he backed away, drawing Brit upward and then down into the water just by following his magnetism. Logan continued backing up until he climbed out of the pool and led the way inside and upstairs to the bedroom.

The next few weeks were going to be trying, so Brit looked forward to the chance to spend some time with just the two of them.

CHAPTER 7

LOGAN WAS going to split into a million pieces, and once he did, he was never going to be whole again. At least that was what he felt like at the moment. Sleep had become harder as the days passed.

"Look, let me give you something to help you sleep," Carlton said as he stood in Logan's living room. It was after midnight, and he was tired to the bone, and yet he knew if he went to bed, he'd lie awake half the night.

Carlton handed him a couple of pills, and Logan stared at them. He had promised Brit that he'd stay away from things like this, but he was too tired to argue. He tossed back the pills, finished his glass, and went up to bed. He fell into a sleep that left him as tired in the morning as he had been the night before. Still, after two cups of coffee, he rode to the studio and went right to wardrobe and makeup, and then onto the set.

"This isn't working," Chris said for the second time. Logan sat down, completely drained. "There's no energy, no interest." He walked up to Logan. "This is one of the big scenes. You've just rescued your son, Harris is threatening the woman you love more than life itself, and you're delivering your lines like you're ordering from a diner menu. Dig down deep and come up with some vitality and excitement."

Logan nodded and turned to Harris, knowing he was fucking this all up. He still didn't like Harris, which was fine. He channeled those feelings into the next take, and his hands shook a little as he threw himself into what he was doing. During a scene, he was always able to ground his focus, but that was missing, and he couldn't make it work. Still, he powered through the scene, sweating profusely by the time it was over. "How was that?"

"Perfect," Chris said, and then they moved on to set up the next shot.

Logan slumped in his chair and wanted to go to sleep. He needed help and wasn't sure what was wrong with him.

Margot brought him some coffee, and he drank half of it, hoping for something to perk him up. "How is Brit doing on his set?" she asked.

"He says he's having the time of his life. The part is great, and he's enjoying what he's doing. They're filming at night, so he sleeps during the day, preps, and then works through the night." The truth was that Logan hadn't actually seen him at all this past week.

"He's a really nice man, and he always appreciates what everyone does for him." She lowered her gaze. "I'm sorry."

"No, please," Logan said, sipping more coffee. It did his heart good to hear someone saying nice things about Brit. Carlton seemed happy that he was gone, though. He hadn't said anything, but the way Carlton slipped back into his old habits told Logan how relieved Carlton was that things had returned to normal from his point of view. "Say what you'd like."

"I'm just an assistant, and no one really sees us most of the time. Brit did. He was nice, and he talked to me even if it was to ask about the day I was having. Harris has been through two assistants already, and Barty is about at his wits' end." She nodded and grew quiet when others came close. Logan figured she didn't want to be caught talking out of turn.

"Thank you for letting me know." Logan liked these tidbits, and it told him that his weren't the only nerves Harris got on.

"Is Brit coming back?" Margot asked.

Logan nodded. "For some of the location shooting in a few weeks." Until then Logan was here alone, and it felt like it. Granted, he was really busy, but after having Brit with him for weeks, the trailer seemed bigger and empty. He missed coming back and running lines with Brit. Logan had thought he'd been helping Brit with his part, and it turned out he was the one helping Logan. Things had flowed with Brit, and he made the work easy. Now, with him gone, everything was tough and it took twice as much effort.

"Is there anything you need?" Margot asked.

"Not right now. Thank you." He inhaled deeply and coughed. "You know, I could really use a shower.

Is there somewhere I can clean up after this next take? I usually go back to the trailer, but…." He leaned closer. "It's like trying to shower in a shoebox." God, he just wanted to spend a few days at home away from all this activity. It seemed like he was running all the time, trying to stay ahead of the jackals on his heels. Brit had a way of keeping all that at bay.

"I think so. Let me see what I can do for you." She hurried away, and Logan sank down and tried to rest a little, but nothing seemed to help.

HIS HANDS shook and his head pounded as he forced his eyes open. He could just make out the ceiling of the trailer. He punched his alarm silent and pushed open the curtains before gazing out into the night. It was a little after five, and he had to be up and ready to go in less than an hour. The problem was that he could barely move. His back ached, his muscles were cramping, and he felt like he was eighty years old. Maybe he was sick. Logan forced himself up and grabbed one of those ear thermometers from the bathroom. He didn't have a fever, but he still felt like shit—and looked even worse.

Logan stripped down, showered in his shoebox, dressed, and checked his phone. He smiled when he saw Brit's message. *This night shooting is something else. It's strange to be working all night and sleeping during the day. BTW, your gardener tells hilarious jokes.*

Good to know. He liked that Brit had gone back to his place.

How are you doing? Is Harris still being a pain?

Logan typed his response. *Everyone hates him and he's a pain in the ass. We're all beyond tired. I'm glad things are going well for you. I have to leave for wardrobe in a few minutes, but I'm glad you texted.* He paused and sent another message. *I miss seeing you.*

Brit sent a smiley face. *I miss you too, but I'll be back in two weeks.* He sent a happy emoticon as well, and some of the tension inside Logan eased. He needed to make it through the next couple of weeks. Knowing that Brit would be there at the end of it helped.

I'm looking forward to it. Even as he sent the message, Logan wondered what he was going to do long-term. If Brit continued on his upward path, it wasn't as though they were going to work together all that often, and he couldn't rely on Brit to prop him up. Logan had to figure out a way to stand on his own two feet. But that was for another time. At the moment, he had to get to wardrobe and then onto the set.

THE DAYS stretched, and clocks seemed to slow to tortoise speed. Logan messaged Brit each day, but he couldn't seem to find a balance. Carlton was with him each morning, and not knowing what else to do, Logan gave himself over to Carlton's ministrations. He ran on autopilot, putting all his energy into filming and doing the very best he could. There were also a ton of tasks that needed his attention, so he split his time between the set, what Carlton needed, and sleeping when he could, which didn't seem to be very often. Still, he soldiered forward until he reached the point where getting out of bed was too much work. His feet felt like lead, and he had no idea what the hell was wrong with him.

Logan sat up, and when his feet touched the floor, they encountered something cold that rolled away from the bed. He rubbed his eyes and opened them again, recognizing his preferred brand of vodka. The thing was, he didn't remember drinking, but he sure as hell knew that dry-mouth, morning-after yuck that clung to his teeth. He got to his feet and turned around as vague memories of the night before began to come back.

Grant had come over with some friends, that much came to him, and they had played in the pool. Logan turned around, almost afraid of what he might find in his bed. Thankfully it was empty. He opened the bedroom door to find the house quiet. That was a blessing. He closed it again and went to the bathroom, started the shower, and stepped under the water. It helped wash away some of the haziness from last night. He remembered the party and maybe some of the guys…. God. He held his head in his hands, forcing his mind to work. Logan felt like shit. Still, he remembered the guys going home and taking their stuff with them. It must have been after midnight.

A frantic knock on the door pulled Logan out of his muddled thoughts. "Thank God I found you." Carlton stuck his head in. "You're due on set in half an hour."

Logan turned off the water, and Carlton passed him a towel. "Lay out some clothes and I'll be right out." He dried himself and shaved quickly, then brushed his teeth. Then he left the bathroom and pulled on the clothes Carlton had set out.

"Here. This will get you going." Carlton handed him a pill and a glass of water. Logan downed it without a thought, stepped into his shoes, and they were quickly out in the waiting car. While they rode, he and Carlton went over the scene he was supposed to film, running lines and reviewing the notes.

"Are you going to be able to do this?" Carlton asked as Logan felt some energy start to return.

"Yes. Just call ahead and tell them I'm on my way. I'll go right to makeup, and they can dress me at the same time." He was coming out of the damned fog. "What the hell happened last night? Do you know?"

Carlton kept his attention on the script in his hand, not meeting Logan's eyes. "I don't really know." Logan got the feeling that Carlton wasn't being truthful. "I threw away the few things I found and left the dishes for the cleaning service to handle." He smiled. "It's a good thing I thought to come by and check on you."

Logan nodded, his mind already shifting to what he was going to have to do. He and Carlton ran the scene again, and this time more of it stuck in Logan's mind. His brain still seemed a little cloudy, but he could get past that and focus on the task at hand. That was what was important. Once the scene was done, maybe he could lie down for a few hours and try to get some more rest.

Logan got through the series of shots before going back to his trailer, where he collapsed on the bed, still in his clothes, after telling Margot to come get him before he was needed. At least he had the presence of mind to remember that.

Logan knew he was out of control, and he had no idea what to do to get it back. He had promised Brit that he wouldn't do this, that he'd hold it together and not fall apart. Instead, he had fallen back into old habits. Just like before, his life was out of control and everything seemed wrong, but he didn't have the energy to do anything about it. Still, he managed to sleep for a time.

"What the hell?" a familiar voice said a little while later, pulling Logan out of his sleep stupor. "Margot, could you please get some black coffee?"

The voice was gentle, and it wrapped around Logan like a blanket. He nestled under the covers, letting the warmth of his dream take him away again. "Logan," the voice said. "It's me." A gentle hand rocked his shoulder.

"Brit?" Logan rolled over. He smiled when he cracked his eyes open. "What are you doing here? I thought you had a few more days of shooting."

"We ran into some scheduling issues, so they brought up some of my scenes and postponed a few others." He sat on the edge of the bed and looked down at Logan. "You look worn out."

"I am. I haven't been sleeping." Logan sat up and rubbed his eyes. "What time is it?"

"Margot said you have forty-five minutes before you're needed." Brit rubbed his hands, and when Logan stood, Brit hugged him tightly. "What happened?" He stepped back, shaking his head. "Let me guess. Carlton was here, and you fell back into your old habits." Fortunately Brit didn't let go of his hand. "You look like you've dropped ten pounds. Have you been eating?"

Logan shrugged. It was hard to remember anything other than scenes and filming. Everything else was a blur.

The trailer door opened, and Margot set some things on the table before leaving again. Brit pressed a cup of coffee into Logan's hands, and once Logan drank some, Brit handed Logan a sandwich. Logan ate, his stomach rebelling against the food, but he managed to keep it down, and after a few minutes it settled. "This is good." Logan took a few more bites and started to feel better.

"What has Carlton been giving you?" Brit's eyes were hard.

"Don't go blaming him," Logan said as he continued eating. "He didn't ram the stuff down my throat. I needed to sleep, and then I needed to be able to wake up so I could perform on set." He set the sandwich on the table.

"Go ahead and eat. You need it." His voice held an edge. "I know you don't owe me anything."

Logan took a few more bites and washed them down with some more coffee. "Shit." He finished the food and then downed the last of the coffee. "I know I promised you... and...."

"I guess it was too much of me to expect," Brit said softly. Logan could read the hurt washing off him. "You were doing so well and you had such confidence. Now I find you in the trailer, looking like hell. The people around you are supposed to help. They're supposed to support you, not pump you full of drugs so you can sleep and then more to wake you up. All that does is...." Brit grew quiet and pulled open the bathroom door. "Look in the mirror. You have huge bags under your eyes like you did when I first met you. You're pale and your eyes are dark. I don't want you to look or feel this way."

And Logan hated that disappointed expression in Brit's eyes. "Like I said, I know I let you down...."

Brit shook his head. "Logan, you let yourself down. That's the person you really hurt and the one who's going to have to pay for all of this." He pulled out a bottle of water and pressed it into Logan's hands. The cold felt good on his skin. "I can't make your decisions for you, and neither can Carlton. All of that has to come from you." Brit stroked his cheek. Damn, Logan had missed the way he did that. In a moment, he felt more present and alive than he had in weeks, and all because of a single gentle touch. "Come on. You need to get back on set." Logan at least felt less like death warmed over, and he left the trailer with Brit.

It was hard for most people to do much other than work while on a movie set. At least it was that way for Logan. It took all his concentration and energy to make it through each day. Since he was the star of the film, he was in nearly every shot, so the movie couldn't progress very far without him. Which meant that while most everyone else got a break during the day, he often didn't.

"I see you're back," Carlton told Brit once the two of them stepped onto the set. "I took good care of Logan while you were gone."

Logan wasn't sure what to make of that comment, but Brit's glare was icy and stayed that way until Carlton took a step back.

"If you're going to be Logan's manager, then I suggest you actually help him. Otherwise find someone who can do the job properly." Carlton smiled like Brit was kidding, but Logan could tell by the set of his jaw that he was serious.

"Carlton, go on back to your office and let me get to work here," Logan said. The last thing he needed was Brit and Carlton arguing on set. "Brit, please."

Logan got into place, and they ran through the scene before they did it for the cameras.

Over and over he raced onto the set and slid across the floor and into what was supposed to be a plate glass window. Somehow it wasn't right, so he kept trying again and again until Chris was happy with it. He went through three sets of trousers during that time and was pleased when his task was done. His hip ached and he'd banged his elbow more than once, but he got the damned shot.

"That's a wrap for today. Crew, have everything set up for tomorrow," Chris called, and Logan limped to where Brit stood.

"I'm ready to go. It's early, and I need some time in the hot tub." Hell, he needed some painkillers.

"Logan, Brit," Chris said as he strode over. "Can I talk to both of you?" From his expression, Logan knew this wasn't going to be good.

CHAPTER 8

"WHAT THE hell is going on?" Chris asked once he got them out of earshot of everyone else.

"Excuse me?" Brit asked, folding his arms over his chest.

Chris remained calm. "The first few weeks of shooting were great. Logan was on top of his game like none of us had seen in quite a while. And don't think I don't know that was because of you. I know you were standing out of shot all day for weeks, regardless of whether you were needed on set. The issue is that the last few weeks have…." He turned to Logan. "You've looked like hell most of the time. Makeup has hidden much of it. But you need to pull yourself together." His expression grew hard. "The producers paid a lot of money to have you in this picture, and they're scared shitless right now."

"Because of me?" Logan asked.

Chris nodded. "Thankfully the scenes we've been doing are needed, but not pivotal to the movie, and you were good enough, but that can't continue. I need you on top of your game or... I hate to say it, but your reputation will relegate you to lower and lower budget romcoms and God knows what else."

Logan nodded. Brit hated seeing Logan's pride taking a beating like this. "I understand that as well as anyone else."

"Good. Then I'm banning your manager from the set. I don't want him here or anywhere on studio grounds. I know what happens on my sets, and I'm well aware that he's been dosing you with uppers and then sleeping pills, and I won't have it. If you need anything, Margot will get it for you. But that man is to stay away."

Brit wanted to agree, but he held his tongue.

"What am I supposed to do?" Logan asked softly.

Chris leaned forward. He was younger than he looked, but those eyes held something whip-smart. "I'd start looking for a replacement. I know you have been together a long time, but he isn't doing you any favors. I can recommend a few people, Margot being one of them. She can be your personal manager if you need one. She's bright and can walk right into those duties."

Brit liked that idea, but he said nothing. One thing he knew—this had to be Logan's decision.

"Regardless, I won't have a drug pusher on my set."

Brit cleared his throat. "I think we need to give Logan a chance to think this over."

Chris nodded. "Next week, we were scheduled to start location shooting, but there's been an issue with

the location. Some sort of plumbing issue that is being
fixed. So after tomorrow, we're going to do the scenic
work. Views of the city and wide exterior shots. Neither of you will be needed. We'll green-screen Logan
in back here." He leaned back in the chair. "Basically,
I'm giving you a week. Go somewhere and get yourself
together. Rest, ride horses, swim, whatever you want,
but sleep and get plenty of rest."

"Where?" Brit asked. He knew immediately that
he needed to get Logan out of the city and away from
everyone here. If he stayed, Grant would bring over the
bikini boys for a party. "We could go to Palm Springs
or something like that."

"I can probably get a house in Malibu for the
week," Logan offered.

Brit shook his head. "We should get away. Some-
place small, quaint, and out of the way. Malibu is where
half of Hollywood lives." He continued thinking.

Chris sighed. "I have a vacation house up north
in Mendocino. It's quiet, nowhere near anything. The
town is small and very much out of the way. No one
will be looking for or suspect a movie star in their
midst." He wrote down the address. "You can have the
house for a week if you like."

"Thanks," Brit told him. "Is that okay?"

Logan seemed a little lost. "What am I going to do
up there?" he asked. "I don't know anything."

"The coast is rugged and amazing. Walk to the
beach, see the lighthouse, explore the town, hike the
redwoods, and above all, get your head on straight.
Nothing will help bring things into perspective like
trees that are hundreds of years old and soar three hundred feet in the air. The air is fresh and clean, and no
one will be looking for you, so just go and let yourself

unwind. When you get back, we'll have all the location shooting and the big stunt scenes. They have to be right." Chris stepped away from both of them.

"You don't have to go if you don't want," Brit offered. "I'm sure we could find somewhere that you'd like better if Mendocino doesn't suit you."

Logan shrugged. "I suppose it will be fine. It's just been a long time since I was away from Hollywood."

"Then maybe it's time. This town tends to warp people. You've seen that. Heck, you've lived it. None of this is real. It's made up. Maybe what you need is some time out in the real world where everything isn't delivered to your door at a moment's notice and where there aren't people hanging around all the time." Brit closed the distance between them. "It will be a whole week of just you and me. We can rest, see the sights." He didn't say it, but he planned to get Logan off those damned pills that Carlton had him on and back on good food, healthy drinks, and an exercise regimen that included being outdoors.

"So what do we do?"

Brit grinned. "How about we go home, pack, and we can leave tomorrow morning? I'll ride to your place, drive home, and we'll meet back at your house and leave in the morning. We can drive up." He was so excited. Having Logan to himself for a whole week was going to be amazing... he hoped.

"THEY CAN'T fucking do that!" Carlton practically screamed as Brit quietly came in through Logan's garage. "Chris has no right to do that." It seemed Logan had delivered the news.

"Actually, they can," Logan said, and God, he sounded completely worn out. "I have a week. Brit and I are going away. I don't want calls or appointments. Reschedule anything that I have. I'm going to rest for a while."

Brit came into the room and set his bag near the outside door. He left Carlton to stew in his own juices before heading upstairs behind Logan.

Logan collapsed on the bed and closed his eyes. "I need to pack." He sighed.

Brit opened Logan's closet and pulled out a Louis Vuitton suitcase that cost more than he made in a month and started filling it with clothes. He kept the wardrobe simple, with jeans and basic slacks. He found some comfy T-shirts, a few sweatshirts, some polos, and a jacket. He added them to the suitcase along with underwear and socks. He also packed some toiletries and other things they might need before closing the suitcase.

"Where are you going?" Logan asked groggily.

"To get Carlton on his way and put our things into that huge-ass SUV you have in your garage. I want you to call your security company and let them know you'll be gone and that no one is to be in the house. We're getting out of here now. Chris gave me the keys and the address. We'll start driving and get out of the city." He had to get Logan away from all of this. Carlton was becoming more of a problem. Brit hoped he was doing the right thing, but he had to try for a change of scenery.

"I'm so tired," Logan whispered.

Brit suspected he was coming down from whatever Carlton had given him. He wanted to wring the man's neck for what he was doing to Logan, but that had to be something Logan did, not him. The thing was, Brit wondered if Carlton thought he was doing the best thing for Logan or if there was more to it. Carlton had rubbed him the wrong way from the start, and the longer he knew him, the more that feeling intensified.

"I know. I'll bring a pillow and things so you can rest in the car. I'll do the driving, and then we'll stop at a hotel and rest for the night." He felt a little like a thief in the night, but he had to get Logan away. That thought kept playing in his head.

"Okay. I'll make the call," Logan said.

Brit went downstairs and walked past Carlton, who was grumping at the counter. He got copies of their scripts and left a message for their agent to let him know what was happening. He left the number that Chris had given him as a contact and then hung up.

"Logan and I are leaving," Brit said, hoping Carlton would take the hint. He just sat there looking at his damned phone. "He's alerting the security company that no one will be in the house, so please arrange for the cleaners to take the week off." He grabbed the bags and hauled them to the garage and set them next to the vehicle. Excitement reigned as he got everything together.

When he came back inside, Carlton was speaking with Logan, who shook his head and then motioned toward the door.

"You handle things here, and be sure to stay on top of what's happening. You can always message me with what you need." Logan ushered Carlton to the door— Carlton talking the entire time—and finally he stepped outside. As soon as Logan closed the door and flipped the lock, he seemed to deflate, the last of his energy gone. "I got the keys." He handed them to Brit, who ushered Logan out to the SUV and gave him one of the nice pillows off the bed, as well as a light blanket. Once he had the car loaded, Brit backed the Lincoln out and started their trek out of Bel Air to the freeway, heading north.

IN THE city, I-5 was busy, but once they reached the base of the pass, traffic eased. By the time they were over the Grapevine, traffic had thinned considerably. Brit set the cruise control as high as he dared, and the miles zipped past on the flat, largely straight road. He found a classical station on Sirius XM and turned it low, and soon Logan fell asleep.

Brit kept driving until about midnight, when he checked them into a hotel. No one saw Logan, and Brit got him in the room and into bed, leaving their luggage just inside the locked door.

"I missed this," Logan said softly as Brit climbed into bed, and Logan wound an arm around him.

"Just go to sleep, and we'll be up and on the road in the morning." Brit closed his eyes, determined to let Logan sleep in as long as he needed to.

What he hadn't accounted for was his own exhaustion. Neither of them woke until nearly nine the following morning. Logan seemed to have more energy, which was great. Maybe the crap Carlton had given Logan was working its way out of his system. Brit got them breakfast at the diner attached to the hotel, and after they ate, he packed the car, and they got on the road again.

A little after noon, they made the turnoff to San Francisco, and an hour later they skirted the city, heading north once again up 101 and then turning off toward the coast. Brit took a few minutes to call Clive and his mom to fill them in on their little adventure so they wouldn't worry about where he was.

"Damn, this is winding," Logan commented as they took yet another set of curves. The dry landscape gave way to huge trees as they entered one of the coastal state parks. All around them, redwoods stretched for the sky.

"But beautiful." Brit pulled off the road and got out. He waited for Logan, took his hand, and wandered a little way off the road, looking up through the tall, straight-trunked trees toward patches of clouded sky. Brit inhaled deeply, letting the quiet of the area soak into him. He could understand why Chris liked it up here. They were alone. No other cars passed either way. "God, I could imagine we're all alone." He leaned against Logan, who put an arm around Brit, sighing.

Brit could still feel the anxiety racing through Logan, but he stayed still, just letting the natural beauty around them slow things down. "How much farther do we have?" Logan whispered. It felt like they were in nature's cathedral, and Brit pressed closer.

"Maybe half an hour or so. Chris messaged that he asked the caretaker to stock the place for us." He smiled. "He's a real good guy."

"He seems solid. Grew up outside Chicago. Parents were blue-collar, worked hard. He went to film school at USC, and the rest is history. He's one of the most grounded in the business." Logan took a deep breath, held it, and released it slowly. Then he led Brit back to the car. "I understand there are hiking trails out here. Maybe we can find one later."

"Definitely," Brit encouraged. If Logan Steele wanted to go hiking and get out into nature, Brit would make sure it happened. He smiled, tilting his head upward. Logan captured his lips, and suddenly everything around them grew silent, drowned out by the sound of his racing heart. Brit wanted to climb Logan right there in the middle of the woods, but he backed away. "Let's go before we end up with dirt in places neither of us wants."

He followed the GPS up the road and then made a right turn near the coast. He lowered the window, letting in the sea air. Up a few miles, he turned left onto a narrow drive and, farther on back on a redwood-forested lot, Brit pulled up to the garage of a small compound.

The buildings had been stained a rustic gray, with decks connecting the main house to what looked like a guest house and other buildings. "Wow, this is something." Brit opened the door and stepped out into the damp air. The marine layer hung overhead, keeping the air cool with a light breeze. After the dry air of LA, this was a treat. Brit handed Chris's keys to Logan and began unpacking the car.

The house was spacious, with natural wood on the walls and thirty-foot ceilings. Skylights and a wall of windows let in natural light.

"Wow," Brit breathed as he set the bags aside. "What a place." He explored and found the master bedroom with its king-size bed all made up and perfectly inviting. Logan helped carry up the suitcases, and then they flopped onto the deep brown leather sofa in the great room, looking out over the cleared yard and redwoods that framed the space.

"It's almost too quiet," Logan said, stretching out.

"Maybe, but can't you feel yourself relaxing by the minute?" Brit asked and went to get them drinks. "Chris wasn't kidding. He had the place stocked to the gills." The freezer was full, as was the refrigerator. Fresh fruit and vegetables as well as juices, and lots of food in the pantry. "We could cook tomorrow."

Logan patted the cushion next to him, and Brit sat down. "I'm just happy not to be in that car any longer. I was going stir-crazy, and that road with the curves? I have never felt motion sick in my life."

Brit chuckled. He had felt it some as well, but at least he'd been driving.

"What do you want to do while we're here?"

Brit grabbed his bag and pulled out their scripts. "I brought these along. I figured we could go through them. And I think we both have messages from Archie," he said. "He doesn't say much other than he's been presented with a script and that he thinks there's something for both of us."

"Thank God," Logan said softly. "I've been worried. Usually I have projects lined up, but after this there'd been nothing." He chewed his lower lip.

"Should I ask him to messenger up the details?" Brit asked.

"I thought we were getting away," Logan teased.

Brit nestled next to him. "I don't know if we ever really can, but some peace and quiet is wonderful. Why don't you call him and see what he's got his fingers into while I start some dinner? After you talk to him, we can finish it together."

Logan rolled his eyes. "I know that means that I need to make the salad." He grinned. "It's all you ever let me do. Though maybe that's for the best."

Brit stayed where he was for a few minutes, soaking up the warmth of Logan and enjoying the quiet. Then he got up to let Logan make his call. He returned after a few minutes.

"Archie is going to overnight the details. He said that there were two really good parts and that he had pitched both of us. Apparently your work on both films has gotten noticed. He said that your dailies have been out of sight and that he's been fielding a number of inquiries." Logan slipped his arms around Brit's waist. "I'd say you're right where you want to be. Just starting out, doing good work, and making a name for yourself."

Brit shrugged. "None of it means anything unless people like me."

Logan shrugged. "That's just it. Right now, you're in the driver's seat. What you're doing is building a reputation for good work, and people are jumping on the bandwagon." He squeezed slightly. "Archie knows what he's doing."

"A lot more than I do." Brit slid out of Logan's arms and took out some chicken and started seasoning it. Then he found some noodles and decided to serve them with a little garlic butter. Finally, they had the salad. That should make a nice, relatively light meal. After all that driving, he didn't want anything too heavy. "What else did Archie have to say?"

Logan paused a second, a little nervous. "Apparently the producers are interested in both of us, but they want you to come in to read for them. The producers have seen some of your dailies, but they want to meet you in person."

Brit shrugged. He had expected something like that. After all, he was new and didn't have a track record. If someone was going to trust a larger, more important role to him, they needed to be confident he could handle it. "What about you?"

Logan came over to where Brit worked in the kitchen. "I don't know. Archie said he was sending the script and made me promise to read it before I formed an opinion. Which means he thinks I'm going to be angry and not like the role at all." He started the salad.

Brit got the chicken in the oven to cook and put a pot of water on for the noodles. "Is it usual for us to be working together like this? I know some people do, but…."

Logan shrugged. "Who knows? Sometimes you see people whose careers closely mirror each other's. But yeah, for now it's probably a little strange, and I'm sure it isn't going to continue. Your career is going to take off. You're talented as hell, and you bring life to the movies you're on. That means a great deal, and people can't help seeing that. Eddie Murphy was a lot like that. He had that smile and that laugh. He could play serious roles and in movies where people got shot, but he had this light that made the movie fun." He topped off the salad, and Brit carried it to the wide plank table while Logan set the table.

They worked together easily. "Should I be worried about coming in to read?"

Logan shook his head. "Nope. It's normal in this business. Just relax and be yourself. Let the energy and sunshine from inside you come forward. If it isn't what they want, then there will be other roles. You've already gotten two of them, and there will be many more. I can feel it." He finished setting the table and sat down, hanging his head slightly.

"What is it?" Brit set the chicken and noodles on the table. "You're not telling me something." He was a little worried.

"Archie said that he isn't getting many calls for me. That *Knockout* and the rumors from on set have really hurt my demand." Brit put his hands on Logan's shoulders and rubbed gently for a minute. "He said that this is a solid offer and that I should think before I make any decisions."

Brit could feel the tension building in Logan's muscles, and he wished he could take it all away. He leaned forward, his lips near Logan's ear. "Just relax. He's sending the script up, and you can read it. Maybe it's as great as he says." He continued stroking Logan's muscles. "Come on. Worrying isn't going to help you, and it doesn't matter. These are just scripts, and I bet you've read a ton of them."

"And a lot of times they never get made anyway," Logan said.

Brit could tell he was stewing, and he went around to his place and made up his plate. "So, eat and let it go," he said. "We'll find out once we get the details, and then we can deal with it." He got up and grabbed a couple microbrews out of the refrigerator and handed one to Logan.

"We?" Logan asked.

Brit sat back down, holding Logan's incredible gaze, which was enough to send a shiver down his back. "If you want there to be a we," he said. "If you want to figure things out on your own, you can do that too." He didn't want to step on Logan's toes. "I'm not going to run your life or tell you what to do. You have enough people who do that." People who gave him pills to get him to perform like some damned monkey in a circus. Brit wasn't going to do shit like that. "But if you want to talk it over and make our decisions together, then we'll do that too." He cut a piece of the chicken and ate it, shaking his head. "Sorry, I think I overcooked it." He got up and rummaged in the pantry, where he found a bottle of chili-ginger sauce. He added a little of that to the chicken, and it helped.

"It's still good," Logan said. "And yes." He lifted his gaze from his plate. "I think I'd like there to be a we."

"Good." Brit took Logan's hand. "I want that too." He grinned and picked up his phone. There was a message from Chris with a link and a passcode for the alarm. He installed it and put in the code. Then he started heating the hot tub in the small gazebo just off one of the decks. He had definite plans for that.

"DO YOU have any idea how many people would give their eyeteeth to be where I am right now?" Brit asked as Logan sank into the hot, bubbling water. He scooted closer and drew Logan to him, sinking them both up to their necks, letting his hands run down Logan's back and then over his bare ass. Damn, the man had an amazing backside, and Brit grew more excited by the second.

"I don't know about that," Logan whispered.

"Come on. Half the women in this country, and a share of the men, would love to have you naked and all to themselves. But you're mine, and I'm going to keep you." Brit brought their lips together, sliding his tongue to duel with Logan's. The heat of the water paled in comparison to the warmth they generated between them.

"Maybe, but none of them are you," Logan whispered.

Brit shook with excitement, and his heart pounded in his chest. No, Brit hadn't said the magic words, because he was afraid of jumping ahead and scaring Logan off. This was probably as close as he was going to get for now, and Brit would take it. Hell, he already knew he was in love with Logan—he had for a while. And that was part of what concerned him. But at the moment, he didn't have the energy to think about such things as Logan laced their legs together, rocking gently, their cocks sliding against each other.

"Have you always been on top?" Brit asked as he slid his hand along Logan's chiseled jaw.

Logan smiled. "Most of the time. It's been a while since I wasn't." His eyes seemed dark and tinged with apprehension. "I really didn't like it."

Brit nodded. "I see."

Logan drew him closer. "The last time I was with someone like that, it didn't go well. He was too… eager, and he hurt me."

Brit held Logan's gaze as all kinds of questions bubbled up in his mind. He didn't want to ask them and risk killing the mood, but he also wanted answers so he could understand. Brit liked to be in control sometimes, and other times he wanted to release that and let someone else have control. He loved the way Logan put Brit's pleasure first. He wanted to give that same thing to Logan.

Brit didn't move, looking deeply into Logan's eyes. "I know what you want."

"Then just give it to me," Brit said with a smile, reaching between them to glide his fingers along Logan's shaft. "And I don't mean that, though I'm sure that can be arranged eventually."

"You're such a tease," Logan countered as Brit gripped him tighter, the heat amazing in his hand.

Brit shimmied slightly. "I'm not a tease. I put out, thank you very much. And just because I'm making you wait a little doesn't mean I'm not going to." He narrowed his gaze. "Nice attempt to change the subject." He knew Logan well enough to know that if something bothered him, the man clammed up. Still, when Logan didn't say anything after a few moments, he groaned. "Sometimes you're just a stubborn ass, you know that? I'm not going to think less of you because someone hurt you or you don't feel comfortable with something. But what worries me is when you won't talk. Holding shit inside only makes it worse."

Logan backed away and sat on the edge of the tub with his legs dangling in the water. "I'm really messed up, okay? I know that. I don't like to talk about shit because I just want to forget all about it." He shivered, and Brit moved between his legs and put his arms around his waist.

"But you can't, can you? No matter how much you try to forget, it always comes back. You can drink all you want to try to calm your nerves and outrun the memories and hurt, but it always comes back." Brit kissed Logan's heated chest. "You don't need to tell me now, because if the truth be told, I have much better use for these amazing lips of yours." Brit kissed him hard, sending the temperature soaring.

"Brit…," Logan sighed.

"Just think about letting go of what you've been holding on to for so long and what's been eating at you to try to forget. None of us can outrun our past. It's always there and always catches up with us." He kissed him again, tugging Logan back into the water. He held his lips, taking possession of them, loving the growl of passion that welled up from inside Logan. God, that sound was sex, pure and wild. It drove Brit higher, and he let Logan press him up against the side of the tub, his weight delicious against him.

"Maybe we can go up to bed," Logan offered, "because if you keep this up, I'm going to fuck you right here and now." His voice was rough and dark with need.

Brit tugged Logan's head closer. "Maybe that's what I want. You've been so gentlemanly and kind, but maybe right now, in this wild place, what I want is for Logan Steele to let go and be the wild man I know you have deep down inside." He kissed him, and Logan lifted them both out of the tub and pressed Brit down on the tile. The ceramic was cold against his back, in stark contrast to the blazing heat that radiated off Logan. Brit's mind cleared just long enough to remember that he hadn't brought any supplies out with him. But it seemed that Logan had thought ahead, and damned if the rip of foil didn't send a shiver through him.

Brit's entire body vibrated in anticipation as Logan got ready. A slick finger breached Brit, and he gasped, so damned ready. Then it was gone, replaced by Logan in all his glory, filling and stretching him in the most amazing way possible. Brit gasped for air as Logan sank deeper. There was no quarter and no letting up. This was intense, with all Brit's synapses firing at once.

"Jesus Christ!" Brit yelled, filling the small space with his passion as he held on to Logan for fear he'd fly in a million directions all at once.

"I have to have you, and I can't wait," Logan whispered in his ear as he pulled out and slammed home once again.

Brit hissed and pressed back, meeting each movement with one of his own. Sweat, musk, and heat mixed with the humid air to create an intoxicating cocktail that, along with Logan pressed over him, drove Brit out of his mind. Everything he wanted was right here, and Brit reveled in the mind-blowing passion as it built more and more, until Brit could take no more and joined the birds above the redwoods.

EVERYTHING WAS so quiet the following morning. They slept late, especially after Brit woke Logan in the middle of the night and climbed aboard, riding him for all he was worth until they collapsed in a sated, sweaty clutch.

Brit loved the silence. He slipped out of bed, cleaned up as quietly as he could, then left Logan to sleep while he dressed in sweats and made a light breakfast. His body ached in all the right places, and about the time he had the food on the table, Logan shuffled down. "I made egg sandwiches. I thought we could take a drive up the coast for a few hours."

Logan looked refreshed, his eyes bright and his smile ready. "I feel great," he whispered. "Better than I have in a long time." There seemed to be no stress, and the dark spots under his eyes had faded.

"Good. Eat your breakfast and have some coffee. Chris told me about a great restaurant in Fort Bragg at the harbor. They have the most amazing shrimp plate, and I can't wait to check it out. And there's a place called Glass Beach where there's tons of sea glass. We can poke around if you like and just enjoy the fresh air. No one is going to be expecting to see you up here."

"But if they do?" Logan asked, taking a bite.

"Then you smile, sign something if they ask you to, and then ask them for a little privacy to enjoy your vacation." It seemed simple to Brit, but he supposed nothing was ever that easy. Still, he thought some time where it was quiet, doing things that normal people did, would help calm Logan's anxiety. "We don't have to worry about all the Hollywood stuff here, and if you are recognized, then just enjoy it and smile. They'll be excited, and that's good." At least he hoped it was.

CHAPTER 9

THE NEXT three days were amazing. They hiked the red-woods, climbed down to beaches covered in bits of glass, and explored inlets carved out by millennia of pounding waves. A few fans had recognized Logan, and he had signed autographs and spent time talking to each one. He caused a mini fracas outside the bookstore, but took the time to say hello to everyone and sent all of the fans on their way happy and smiling. The thing was, they were so happy to see him that he got caught up in their excitement.

"Who is that?" Brit asked as he pulled up to the garage at the house, passing a parked car Logan didn't recognize. Not that he paid all that much attention. "Are you expecting anyone?" He turned off the engine and checked his phone. "There's nothing from Chris, though it could be a friend of his who saw someone was here." They got out and walked around to the back door. It was locked, and no one seemed to be there.

Logan went inside and found the rooms empty, but when he turned back toward Brit, Carlton strode in.

"What are you doing here?" Logan snapped before he could stop himself. He had gotten into a mindset where Hollywood and the rat race it represented were hundreds of miles and eight hours away. He could forget about them. And now they just came striding through the damned door. "I didn't ask you to come."

"There are things that we need to go over. I tried calling, but I didn't get an answer, so I got worried. Damn, that's a long drive from San Francisco." He pulled out a chair.

"Make yourself at home," Brit commented with no small amount of sarcasm.

"I found this outside waiting for you." Carlton held up a FedEx envelope, and Brit took it and set it aside without opening it.

Logan sat down as well. "Why are you here? I came here to get away from everything. I need some peace and quiet, and I'm feeling good right now. I only have a week away."

"Archie has a script for you to read, and he wanted to make sure you didn't prejudge the part." Carlton looked over at Brit, who had held up the package. "Oh, I see." Once Carlton turned away, Brit half stomped out of the room, leaving the two of them alone.

Logan leaned forward. "Okay. It's time you put your cards on the table. What are you really doing here? And don't give me any bullshit. I'm not in the mood for any Hollywood smoke screen. I've only been away four days, and you drove all this way... for what?

To tell me about a script that's been delivered? Is there anything else that I don't know? We have email—you could have sent one." Something was rotten in Denmark, and Logan intended to get to the bottom of it.

Carlton's eyes grew hard, and his lips formed into a straight line. "If you must know, it's Brit. You met him, what, six, eight weeks ago? You get him a part in your movie, and now he's getting more parts, an audition for a starring role, and he's got you up here away from everyone. I think he has way too much influence over you. I mean, we have been working together for five years, and suddenly I'm on the outside." He sat back, crossing his arms over his chest. "What am I supposed to think? Your friends are worried too. He comes into your life, and suddenly everything is different. You used to have fun with Grant and the guys, and now they aren't welcome. You've sidelined me from your life, and I'm only good enough when *he's* not around."

Logan sighed. "Look, Brit is my boyfriend, and you need to get used to that." He didn't want to have a big blowup. Already his anxiety was spiking, and it had taken days for him to get to the point where he didn't feel like he was on the verge of a headache every minute of the day.

Carlton glared. "And what's with Chris saying I'm not allowed on set? Other assistants and personal managers are there all the damned time."

Brit came down the stairs and immediately came up behind Logan and put his hands on Logan's tense shoulders. "It's okay," he said gently. "If you want to lie down, I'll explain things to Carlton."

Logan was so tempted. He hated these kinds of confrontations. But this was his to deal with. "It's simple. Chris won't have a pill-pusher on his set, and that's what he thinks you are." Logan just put it out there.

"He isn't blind, and he knew I was taking uppers in the morning and then something to sleep at night. The thing is, I'm sure you thought you were helping me, but it was only making me more anxious and jittery all the damned time. So then I'd drink to calm down, and when I needed energy, there was Red Bull...." He felt his chest tightening, and Brit kneaded his shoulder for a few more seconds and then got him some water.

"Just drink. It's okay. I'm sure Carlton is a big enough person that he can handle the truth and will be able to understand that things need to be done differently." Damn, Brit was so calm, and the knot in Logan's belly started to unwind. "Is there some other reason you're here?" Brit asked. "Because if not, then I suggest you start the drive back to the city before it gets too late."

"What?" Carlton asked, his voice rising.

Brit was so calm. "You have work to do, I believe, and you aren't going to get it done here. And if you think you're going to barge in here and then stay, you're out of your mind." He tossed his cell phone on the table. "This is a phone. You call people or send a message. You don't travel halfway up the state without using one first." Man, he could be pissy.

"Well...," Carlton huffed and then turned to Logan. "Is this what you want?"

Logan sighed, suddenly tired. "What I wanted was a week of quiet and peace. Now I have you here making demands and acting like a diva with an out-of-joint nose when you get called out for barging in uninvited." He didn't say any more, but Carlton finally took the hint and got up, heading for the door.

"I only ever wanted what was best for you," Carlton said.

Logan blew out his breath. "That sounds to me like you're giving notice." Chris's words about Carlton ran through his head. Maybe Carlton wasn't helping him.

Carlton stopped dead in his tracks. "Should I?" he asked.

Logan could tell he was hurt. But Carlton hadn't been helping him as much as Logan thought. Though they had been together for five years, through a lot of success, this felt like the end of a long road.

He stood. "I don't know. But it seems like you and I aren't on the same page any longer." The earth under Logan's feet had turned to quicksand, and he wasn't sure what he wanted to do. Maybe Chris was right and he needed someone else. Carlton hadn't been very good for him lately. More like playing into Logan's insecurities and worries instead of helping him. But he didn't want to turn his back on years of work and trust.

"How about this?" Brit offered. "Carlton, you go back to LA, and the two of you think about things and don't make any decisions now."

Logan tilted his head slightly. He had thought Brit would be happy to have Carlton gone. This suggestion took him by surprise, and he wondered what was going on.

"Why? So you can fill Logan's head with whatever you two have going? I don't know what you're after or what you think you're going to get." He grew rigid.

"Carlton, that's enough. Brit hasn't asked me for anything. Nothing at all. He doesn't take money, and believe it or not, he pays his own way, unlike most people I know." Logan swallowed. He needed to bring this to an end. "Go back to LA. I'm fine, and I'm an adult who can make his own decisions. I'll talk to you when I return to the city at the end of the week." That was the sensible thing to do.

"Fine." Carlton left the house, closing the door with more force than necessary.

Brit groaned and sat down across from Logan, taking his hand. "Do you want me to go get him? We can set him up in one of the guest rooms for tonight and he can leave in the morning."

Logan closed his eyes, enjoying the simple touch. "I don't know. I think sending him back is mean, but we didn't ask him to come, and now he's just showed up, and…. Yeah, go get him. We can put him up for the night… but we're damned well going to make sure he doesn't get any fucking sleep."

Brit grinned. "How about we let him sleep, and we do the fucking?" He got up from the table and went to the door, stepping outside as Logan tried to get his anxiousness under control. He hated feeling this way. He used to be so confident, so sure of himself. There had always been this well of energy inside, but for the last year or so, it had been dry. The worst part was that he didn't know what to do about it or how to make the well start filling again.

"Where is he?" Logan asked when Brit returned.

"He drove out fast enough that he spun around the curve going around the bend. I waved to him, but he kept going." Brit closed the door. "How about we…?"

"Just come here and sit," Logan whispered.

Brit pulled out the chair next to him, and Logan leaned against him, their shoulders touching. It was just enough to calm some of the jitters he wished he didn't have. Just a touch made him feel better.

"I'm not going to tell you what I think you should do," Brit told him. "That's something you have to decide for yourself. But I think…." He trailed off.

"What?" Logan asked with more snap in his voice than he intended. Brit shook his head.

"It's fine. You don't need my two cents," Brit said.

Logan huffed, his nerves on edge. "Just tell me. Everyone seems to have a damned opinion on shit in my life lately. Chris, Carlton, you... I'm sure Grant has one too. Hell, Margot probably has opinions on what I should be doing." He got to his feet. "Maybe Harris has one, and I can go find out what *he* thinks I should be doing."

Brit's eyes widened. "You know, we only want to help you."

Logan shook his head. "Everyone wants to control me. They want me to act the way they want and do the things they want. Grant loves to come over with his friends or the guys so he can show off the fact that he's friends with a movie star. Carlton wants to be the one to make my decisions and tell me where to go and how to act. And you...."

Brit stood, stepping closer so they were toe-to-toe. "What is it you think I want from you?" He crossed his arms over his chest, puffing himself up, gaze as hard as flint, lips straight. Logan would have thought his intensity sexy as hell if it weren't for the anger in his eyes. "Because I'll have you know that I don't want anything from you." He leaned closer. "That's not true. I want you to take fucking care of yourself... I want you to stop taking the damned pills and all that shit. Most of all I want you to be fucking happy, and I want to be happy too, dammit. And maybe, just maybe, I'd like a few days where there aren't people like Carlton pulling at us. So yeah, find someone to replace Carlton. If Chris sees something wrong, then so do others, including producers and other directors. People talk."

Part of Logan wanted to argue, but he had nothing. Instead, he plopped himself down in the chair. "I really fucked things up, didn't I?" It was like the tide was coming in, and he had no way to get to higher ground. Still, Brit didn't need this. He had already put up with enough of Logan's crap. Logan wondered how long Brit was going to stand for it before he decided Logan wasn't worth the aggravation.

"Hey." Brit leaned close and held him tightly. Logan noticed he didn't deny it, but he hadn't pulled away either. "Half the battle is admitting that there's a problem. Once we do that, then steps can be taken to fix it. One of them you're doing right now. You've worked hard on *The Anti-Assassin*, and it's showing. Chris wouldn't have let us borrow his place if he thought you were totally out of control."

Logan patted Brit's hand and stood. Maybe what he needed was some time alone to try to figure some of this shit out. He had always been more of a "go with his gut" kind of guy, and now it seemed those instincts were leading him in the wrong direction, and the path back was obscured by so much brush, he couldn't find his way. "That's easy to say."

"Of course it is," Brit said. "I lived the same turmoil you're experiencing. My father was terrible, and he brought complete chaos into the house. I had no idea if I was going to get sober-and-fun dad or drunk-and-mean dad. So I always assumed he was the bad one and tried to stay away from him, which only made the situation worse. I guess he and Mom just weren't good together, because apparently he was different once he left and remarried. Or maybe his new wife didn't take his crap. I have no idea."

Logan narrowed his gaze. "Then I have to ask why you have anything at all to do with me. I have so many of the same issues your father had. I'm a fucking mess."

"I've asked myself the same question," Brit said. "And I think the difference is that I know you'd hurt yourself before you'd hurt me." He leaned closer, the heat from his skin reaching Logan's. His eyes held so much more meaning than his words, and Logan wished he could parse all of it. And yet maybe the answer he was looking for was right there, because whenever he looked into those deep blue eyes, he saw something he might have been looking for his entire life.

Long ago Logan had learned that sometimes there were no words. Hell, even when the lines were in front of him on the page, the real meaning behind them could sometimes be found in the eyes, and Brit's were so damned expressive and open.

Brit didn't hide stuff, at least not with Logan—not when it came to his expression. He was open and honest, something rare in his world, and Logan wanted to hold on to that, and to Brit, with everything he had. There was so little in his life like that. He worked and lived in a world of false fronts, sets, and make-believe. Brit was anything but.

"When you look at me, what do you see?" Logan asked, almost unable to believe he'd had the courage to say the words.

"I see you," Brit answered barely above a whisper. "I always have."

In that moment, Logan realized he was in love with Brit… and had no idea what the hell to do about it. His first instinct was to take him up to the bedroom they were using, but for some reason it didn't feel right. Not that he didn't want to, but he felt off—*sex* at this moment felt off.

"Logan… it's not all that complicated." Brit smiled that quirky smile that said he thought Logan was being a little nutters. "I see you for the man you are. Nothing more or less."

"Okay."

"And what do you see when you look at me?"

It was a fair question, and Logan swallowed damned hard, because the words that came to mind seemed so flat and ordinary. Brit was none of those things, but every time he tried to express what he wanted, it didn't sound right in his head. "Logan?" Brit asked when the silence between them stretched on. "You must feel something…."

Logan nodded. "What I feel and see is too much," he admitted. "There aren't words."

Brit leaned closer. "Then show me." He captured Logan's lips in a bruising kiss hard enough that Logan nearly tumbled off the chair. He would have if he hadn't held on to Brit, who clutched him close as energy coursed through both of them. That earlier reluctance, that feeling of insecurity, vanished in an instant. This was perfection, what he needed more than anything. And when Brit pulled back and took his hand, drawing Logan to his feet, he let Brit lead him to the bedroom.

Brit stripped off Logan's clothes and pushed him onto the bed with enough force that he bounced slightly on the mattress. Brit stood at the end of the bed, still dressed. "A million people would give a ton to see the view I have right now. But it's mine… all mine, and not for anyone else ever." He pulled his shirt over his head, and Logan's mouth went dry at the sight.

"Fuck, I want you," Logan groaned before he could stop the words.

Brit stilled like he'd been transformed into marble. "Is that what you want? Do you trust me enough?" he breathed.

Logan realized what he'd said and what Brit was asking as he nodded and sat up, stroking his hands over Brit's sleek chest.

"Yes, I do." Those words were as close to *I love you* as he would allow himself to get right now.

Brit wound his fingers through Logan's hair, his scalp tingling at the touch. Brit kissed him hard, somehow managing to get out of his shoes and the rest of his clothes. Then he pressed Logan back down on the bed, straddling him for a few minutes as he lavished attention on him to the point that Logan could barely breathe.

"What is it you like?" Brit asked him.

Logan chuckled. "You know, we have done this before."

Brit rolled his eyes. "Okay. Let me ask this. Close your eyes and think of your deepest, most closely held fantasy. The one you hold tightly because it might scare you a little. The one that won't leave your head, even if it does scare you." He leaned closer, and Logan shivered. "I think you know what it is."

"I dreamed about having someone I trusted enough to be able to be myself with." The thought scared him and thrilled him. Up until now, he hadn't been sure he'd ever be able to let his control, his defenses, down far enough to allow that. Not that he didn't remember a time when it had been good, because damn, his first time had been special.

"Is it that simple? There's nothing else?" Brit asked as he nuzzled Logan's neck. "Remember there's nothing that can shock me. I spent months watching other guys fuck in front of a camera. There were positions and scenarios that sent chills through me because, like… no way was that for me. But you aren't going to shock me."

Logan understood. "Maybe I don't want to shock myself." He tugged Brit closer. "Some things like that are best kept locked away because when they get vocalized or see the light of day, they vanish like the mist." He blinked, and Brit nodded slowly. Then he kissed him again, adding more passion to the fire that already burned between them.

"Then we'll take things one step at a time," Brit said, setting Logan into shakes of anticipation. "You know I would never hurt you."

Deep down, he accepted that as a fact. Brit might be forceful at times and exuberant in his passion, which was exciting as hell, but he would never cause Logan pain. The fact that he knew that so deeply was a surprise and sent Logan's heart soaring.

Brit backed away and hurried to one of the dressers, where he fumbled with some things before returning and setting supplies on the bedside table. "We're going to take this slow," he whispered as he slipped his fingers down Logan's thighs, teasing him and then backing away only to slip downward once again.

"Brit…." Logan gasped.

"Just relax. This is going to feel so good," Brit crooned, his tone deepening and sending ripples of passion racing beneath Logan's skin. Logan could bask in the glow of Brit's gaze for the rest of his life with no complaints and no need to be anywhere else. Brit felt like home to him, welcoming and special in a way that filled a place in his heart he hadn't known was empty.

It had been a long time since he had allowed anyone to touch him in one of his most private places, and damned if Brit didn't know how to put him at ease with his gentle firmness and steady hands, teasing and touching. Brit watched him so intently that Logan was afraid he could see his deepest and darkest secrets. Yet if they were open to Brit, he didn't care. Not at a moment when Brit was taking him to a place of such heated pleasure. Not when Logan was filled, Brit's digits sliding over a spot inside that sent Logan's eyes rolling to the back of his head, sweat breaking out all over, breaths hard to take because it required effort better suited to paying attention to what Brit was doing to him.

"Is this going to be okay?" Brit's lips were so close to Logan's they shared breath, and Logan inhaled what Brit gave him. He had never experienced that connection before, and damn, he hoped it continued forever.

Brit slowly pressed forward. Logan tensed initially and then let Brit in, stretching as he pushed back, taking in Brit's heat, joining their bodies and hearts, continuing a tender dance that humans started millions of years before.

Suddenly Logan was part of something so much larger than himself. He was with Brit—part of him, if temporarily, and yet part of the cosmos, the entire human experience of not just the act of sex, but of deep, unabating human love. The emotion that brought two people together and connected them with the rest of the human race as lovers that existed now and centuries in the past. Logan had never considered himself a poet and would probably forget these thoughts, but maybe if they stayed with him once their passion was spent, he'd write them down and give them to Brit.

"Jesus…," Logan whispered as he snapped back to Brit like a breaking rubber band. His thoughts flew out of his head, and all that remained was Brit's gaze shining down at him and the way his entire body seemed on fire with desire for the man he loved. "Don't stop."

"I won't," Brit breathed. "I'm not hurting you, am I?"

"As you said to me once, I'm not made of glass," Logan growled, and yet Brit simply kissed him and continued his almost agonizing pace. Now that he had broken through his own barrier, he wanted more, and yet Brit simply held him steady, gazing from above him, cobalt flecks dancing in his eyes.

Logan hoped this contentment and happiness never ended. For the first time in his life, he had everything he wanted right at the moment, right here. This was the epitome of happiness, and Logan intended to hold on to it for as long as he could. He was well aware that this kind of heart-pounding joy was fleeting, so he threw himself into the passion between then until they both flew together… but still, a small part of him knew the realities of the earth below were waiting.

CHAPTER 10

BRIT WENT through the checkout line at the grocery store in Fort Bragg the following morning and paid for what they needed. Logan had been on edge through dinner and into the evening. Brit had thought that wearing him out in the best way possible might take away some of his anxiousness, and it did for a while, but the calm and quiet of the earlier days seemed to be gone, and Brit didn't know how to bring back that peace. He wanted to smack Carlton for showing up at all.

"Your total is $58.20," the cashier told him.

Brit inserted his card in the reader. "Thank you." He packed up the food in the reusable bags he'd found in the house and left the store. Once in the car, he went through a drive-through to get a drink and then headed back.

About two miles from the driveway, traffic came to a stop, with people milling about in the road. Brit put the car in Park and turned off the engine before wandering up to see where a full-size redwood had fallen across the road, its trunk nearly as tall as he was.

"Looks like no one is going anywhere soon," a woman groused as she turned back toward her truck.

"I called emergency and they said they were sending someone," a man said as he shoved his phone in his pocket. "Don't know how long it will be. They're going to have to get a huge truck and a lift in here to move this."

"Is there any way around it?" Brit asked.

"I'm looking at maps," another said. "I think if you go back half a mile and turn right, there's a road that looks like it goes through and passes this by. I'm going to check it out." He returned to his car, did a three-point turn, and went back the way he'd come. Brit stayed put, figuring if it didn't work, he'd be back.

After a half hour, when no one showed up and the man who left didn't return, Brit got tired of wandering the area and returned to the car, turned around, and headed off. He found the turn and started around. The road grew narrow, barely more than a single lane. He hoped to hell no one came the other way. Slowing, he continued forward until he reached a crossroad. His phone had no signal, but he hoped he'd gone far enough. He turned toward the main road, where he came on the backup of folks heading north. He turned and continued away from the fallen tree as a group of vehicles started toward the way he'd come. What a pain, but he'd made it. He pulled into the drive and grabbed the groceries before heading inside.

"Logan?" he called as he put the bags on the counter.

A crash from the bedroom had Brit racing up the stairs and into the room, where he found Logan standing near the bed, a broken glass on the floor, a red-covered script facedown on the bed.

"Do you know what these assholes have done?" he asked, slurring his words slightly as the scent of whiskey reached Brit's nose.

"Let me clean up the glass. Then you can tell me," Brit said, breathing through his mouth, trying to calm himself. He stomped down to the pantry and got the broom and dustpan before returning to the bedroom to sweep up the glass and clean up the spilled alcohol from the floor before it stained.

"They have a supporting role for me," Logan snapped while Brit got the glass in the dustpan. "A stinking supporting role. That's all they want me for. I called Archie, and he said that was all he could get for me. But that it was a good part." He flopped on the side of the bed and reached for the whiskey bottle on the table.

Brit snatched it away. "Did you actually read the script for *Over the Moon*? Or did you look at the size of the role and get yourself all worked up before reaching for a damned bottle?" He took the broom and full dustpan out of the room along with the whiskey bottle. He threw away the trash and hid the bottle under the sink.

"I don't need to read it. I'm a movie star. I get starring roles and top billing, not supporting actor shit." When Logan started down the stairs, his legs flew out from under him and he ended up sliding the rest of the way down on his ass.

"What did Archie say? He said to read it before you judged the part. But no." Brit stormed over as Logan tried to get up. Instead, Brit pressed him back down on his butt. "You had to go get drunk and wallow in your own self-pity. Is this what things are going to be like? You getting upset, drinking yourself into oblivion, and then me picking up the pieces?" Brit could barely see straight as the true impact of the decisions he'd made as far as Logan was concerned came into view.

"What am I supposed to do?" Logan asked, attempting to get up a third time and succeeding, but only barely. Brit wondered how much he'd had to drink in the two hours he'd been gone.

"What do you think? Look at things logically, take things one step at a time, and really evaluate them. You don't need to reach for a damned bottle whenever you get upset." He stalked closer. "Or do you? Is the urge to drink so strong that you would rather have that than me? Than your career... the people who truly care about you? Is that what you want? Because I can tell you from personal experience that drinking to drown out your fears and to try to make the world feel better does not work." His heart raced, and he felt heat building behind his temples.

"Do you have any idea how much of an embarrassment this will be if I do this?" Logan asked.

Brit drew closer. "Embarrassment? Do you want to talk about that? How about coming back home after getting groceries in town to find the man I love drunk off his ass because his part isn't fucking big enough? What the hell happened to you? Did someone chop off your goddamned balls? You couldn't wait to talk about this with me. Nope. Instead you reach for the damned bottle and that's it. Bury your hurt and anger in alcohol." He shook his head. "I need to get the hell out of here before I—"

"What?" Logan demanded.

"Before I say something I can't take back." Brit hurried over to where Logan wobbled on his feet. He got him into one of the chairs. "My father ruined our family with alcohol. Maybe it was because he wasn't happy with my mother and me." He swallowed around the orange-sized lump in his throat. "Maybe I wasn't good enough and he drank, and then when he left and had a different family, he was a different person."

Logan shook his head before groaning. "That's bullshit. Your father drank because he drank. He chose to, just like I did when…." He stopped and moaned softly, bringing his head forward to rest it on his hands. "He drank because it was an easy escape. He wasn't fucking happy, so he drank." Logan stared unfocused toward an old movie poster of *Casablanca* on the wall.

"Is that what you are—unhappy? Do I make you unhappy, like I may have done to my father?" Brit put it out there.

"No." Logan pulled him close, his voice hoarse. "You do just the opposite, and I opened the damned script, and you weren't here, and…." He buried his head against Brit's shirt. "I need help," he whispered.

Brit closed his eyes and lifted his gaze skyward. "Then we'll get you what you need." He closed his arms around Logan. Gently, Brit got Logan back up on his feet. "Come on, let's get you upstairs so you can lie down." Somehow, he got Logan into the bedroom. He took off his own shoes and then fell onto the bed.

Logan got comfortable and then closed his eyes before propping his arms up under him. "Will you be here when I wake up?" He extended one hand, and Brit took it. "You won't just leave me, will you?" Brit shook his head. "And it wasn't just the whiskey, was it? Did you actually say you loved me?"

Brit settled Logan on the bed. "Rest. I'll still be here… and yes, I love you." He kissed Logan on the forehead, and Logan closed his eyes. God help him, Brit did love the man, and now he was going to pay the piper. Brit just hoped it didn't cost him too much.

BRIT WAS scared, and damn it all, his mother was right. He thought he had gone into this with his eyes open, and he had, to a degree. But was he a complete fool for thinking he could help Logan? Maybe he had helped some, or maybe he was just fooling himself. Logan had made a step forward by admitting that he needed help, and Brit would help him get what he needed. But there was more to this than Logan's drinking. Okay, so he got upset and hit the bottle. People did that sometimes. Not that Brit didn't recognize that Logan's issues went deeper than that. And he understood what the source might be.

Logan was a movie star. He'd worked his way to the top, and it was hard to stay there. The pressure would get to anyone, and Brit wondered at the people he'd surrounded himself with. They weren't helping him at all. Brit quietly went upstairs and peeked into the bedroom where Logan was sleeping. After making sure he was okay, Brit returned to the living room. He called Clive, but it went to voicemail, so then he called the only other person he could talk to about something like this.

"Honey, how is the shooting going?" his mom asked as soon as she answered. "Are you going to be a big star?" The excitement and pride in her voice warmed Brit's heart. "How is Logan? Are you still seeing him?" And there was her skepticism and the lion he knew.

"Yes, I'm still seeing him. Remember, he and I are on a break this week." He took a deep breath. "The director loaned Logan his house, so we're up in Mendocino." Brit lowered his voice. "Mom, I think I need some help."

She sighed. "I've been expecting this call. What's happened?"

Brit hesitated and then told her about being away, Logan using pills, and then the drinking and his reaction to the script. "I don't know what to do," he whispered. "Logan told me that he needs help, and I know that's the first step and all. But I'm scared. I don't want to go through what you went through with Dad. But…."

His mom humphed. "Okay, first thing. I don't see your father in Logan. He and I were young, too young, and I got pregnant because the two of us were stupid. Then I lost the baby and the next three, until I was able to carry you." Her voice grew rough. "I thought I loved him, and looking back, I think I really did. He loved me, and we got married and started a life… then had you. That was the highlight of our lives together. But it wasn't enough. We were so young…." He could almost see her squirming in her chair. "I'm not making excuses for your father. He had his issues and still does. His drinking compounded our problems, and he was a mean drunk. But there were other issues. Deep ones. And yes, he met someone younger and left." She sniffed, and Brit thought she might be crying. "But none of that had anything to do with you."

"Then my father rarely seeing me after he left…," Brit said.

"He didn't see either of us. He moved halfway across the country, and he had started a new life. Yeah, it was a shitty thing to do to both of us." She inhaled deeply.

"Are you smoking?" Brit asked after she inhaled.

"Yes. I'm out on my patio." She coughed. "Okay, I put it out. Filthy habit, but there are times when I want one badly, and talking about your father makes me wish I could smoke a joint and forget about everything but the best parts. And sweetheart, you are the bestest of those parts. Your father and I were a mistake that we made when we were young. And I think his drinking was part of that mistake. But I don't know. I wish he had tried to cope differently."

Brit found himself nodding. "So you think Logan is just trying to cope?"

"I don't know. I wish I had an answer for you, and I wish to all hell that you weren't going through this the way I did. But I have some questions for you. If you love him, and if you think him asking for help is truthful and honest, then… follow your heart. Your father never asked for help… not once." She took a sharp breath, and Brit leaned forward in the overstuffed chair he was sitting in. "But…."

"What?" Brit asked.

"This is something that Logan has to do for himself, and it's going to be hard. He seems like a very nice man, and it was apparent to me that he cares for you a lot. Just the way he watched you when you walked into the room, I could see that man adores you. I know that. But nothing is ever perfect. I just wish you weren't going through all this."

Brit swallowed hard. "Me too. But I love him, Mom. That's what worries me. I love him so much, and he's good to me and listens to me." Most people would think that Logan helping him would be why Brit loved him, but that had nothing to do with it. Yeah, it was nice and it had shown Logan's kindness, but it was so much more than that. It was the way Logan looked at him and how he treated him. The way Logan held him at night when he was asleep… like Brit was precious and needed to be protected. And maybe that was what they both understood. In a world that was harsh and sometimes cold as hell, Brit instinctively tried to protect Logan from it… and Logan seemed to do the same. "But is it enough?" He hadn't realized he'd asked the question out loud.

"I can't answer that for you. That's something you have to answer for yourself. But I'll be here to listen if you need me. But look, what happened between your father and me is our mess. He and I created it, and we lived with it for longer than we should have. And there were good times too. It wasn't all bad."

"Are you trying to make me feel better?" Brit asked. "I would have thought you'd tell me to go running for the hills after everything you went through. When we talked at the house, you warned me about exactly what's happened." He was a little confused. He had called his mom for a cold dose of reality and gotten something different. Not that he was complaining.

"Sweetheart, I can't make your decisions for you. If you're asking me, then yes, I wish you had fallen in love with a cute, sweet, loves-you-to-death accountant. But you didn't. Instead, you met and came to love a man with passion—an artist. He's an actor just like you, and let's face it, not everyone is as strong as you or as determined. We all have our flaws, and if you can love someone despite their flaws and they are willing to love you back, knowing yours, then…."

Brit chuckled, because this was not at all what he had expected. If he was honest with himself, his mother might have done an "I told you so," but she didn't. At least not so far. "Thanks for your support and for being honest."

"I try. It's easy to look back on what happened and only remember the bad things and paint your father with a single brush. I'll admit that I did that for a lot of years."

"What's changed?" he asked, leaning back and getting comfortable. He really loved this place, with the quiet, and just looking out the window brought to mind how small their problems were in the grand scheme of things.

"Well… when you get back into the city and have an evening free, there's someone I'd like you to meet. His name's Paul Barringer, and he's an accountant." The two of them shared a laugh.

"Logan and I will be coming back on Saturday, so maybe we could get together on Sunday for lunch or dinner. I'm not sure which, but I'd like to meet Paul. Do the two of you want to come to the house? Going out can get to be a little dramatic if Logan is there." And Brit was hoping he would be. He really wanted him to be part of the family. "How long have you and Paul been seeing each other? How did you meet?"

"I met him on one of those online dating things. Betty Wilson—you remember her from up the street?— she helped me get signed up, and I liked him, so I swiped the thing, and we went out about four months ago. I've been seeing him since then. It's been nice, and I like him."

"Why didn't you tell me earlier?" Brit asked her.

"Because I wasn't sure. Paul's wife passed away from cancer three years ago, and it took a lot for him to put himself out there. I spent a lot of years alone. We wanted to take our time and see what happened. But I think he's getting serious, so I want you to meet him." Brit couldn't blame her. She had dated a few times after Dad left, but she didn't seem to have much luck. Part of that was having a teenager at home, and Brit was always grateful to her that she'd put him first. But it was time she put herself first now, and Brit hoped this Paul made his mom happy… or else.

"Okay. I'd love to meet him."

"Good. But no 'if you hurt my mom' speeches. It would be cliché considering I got one from his daughter when I met her last week." This was serious, then— his mom and Paul were at the "meet the kids" stage. That was good.

"Just be happy." He stood and went to sit on the sofa, put his feet up, and stared out the window into the woods with trees that soared to the sky. "I'll call you when we know when we'll be arriving home."

"Great. I'll talk to you then." She hung up, and Brit set his phone on the table and grabbed the script with bent pages that Logan had been reading. He found the half-crumpled letter from Archie shoved inside. After reading that, he straightened out the pages and settled in to read.

BRIT WAS blinky when he heard Logan on the stairs. "Feeling better?" Brit asked as he glanced at the final page of the script and set it on the table. "Get yourself some water and come over here. I'll make a light dinner in a little while. But I think you and I need to have a talk."

Logan groaned. "Not another one."

"No. Not a fight this time, but a real talk. No yelling, and each of us will remain calm." He was so damned excited he could barely sit still. But he waited until Logan joined him with a bottle of water. "I read this, and I think you need to as well. Put your ego aside and just read the entire thing."

"Why?" Logan snapped, and Brit hit him with a cold stare. "Sorry." He flopped down and drank some more.

"Because this is damned good. I want to be Diego. Hell, I can already feel him and have him figured out. The guy speaks to me deep down. I sent a message to Archie to set up whatever these people want and to do it now. But that's me, and this is the chance of a lifetime."

"For you. This is just a slippery slope downward for me."

Brit picked up the script and thrust it at Logan. "Did you read it?" He pushed it into Logan's hands. "I suggest you do, because this is one of those parts that is so beefy and so good, it's stunning. This movie, if it actually gets made, will be one that moves people. And the role, the one you're grousing about… no, it isn't the lead, but it's Mercutio for *Romeo and Juliet*, or Whoopi Goldberg for *Ghost*. This role makes the damned movie, and you will be stunning in it, so read the damned script and quit complaining."

Brit left the room. Sometimes, like in the theater, you had to know when to make an exit, especially when it came to making a point.

CHAPTER 11

THE TRIP home was long, and Logan was happy when they pulled into the drive late Saturday night and he could get out of the car. His legs ached and he needed to move. He could deal with that, but the way things had changed with Brit bothered him. Logan couldn't quite put his finger on it, but Brit wasn't as open, and he seemed… not distant, but more reserved. The worst part was that Logan couldn't blame Brit. It was all Logan's fault. He had let his stubbornness, anger, stupidity, and his damned ego get the better of him.

Logan got his bag and went inside, turning off the alarm.

"Are we still having dinner with your mother?" Logan asked. Maybe Brit wouldn't want him to come.

"If you want to, yes," Brit answered softly. "I'll find out where and when to meet and message you." He left his bag by the front door.

"You're leaving?" Logan asked, a tinge of panic rising in his belly. He had to try to explain things to Brit, to figure out a way to make this right. As it was, the world was a little off-kilter, and Logan had to fix it.

Brit nodded. "I think we've spent an entire week together, and maybe the two of us need some time apart. I know I have things I need to think about, and I'm sure you do too." He kissed Logan, but it was chaste and held none of the heat his kisses usually did. "I'll see you tomorrow." Brit squeezed his hand and then left, backing his old car out of the drive, leaving Logan in the house alone. It would have been so much easier if he and Brit had fought—at least he could argue back. But this was something he couldn't fight and didn't know how to fix.

It felt strange to be in his own house without anyone else. He had everything—pool, pool house, exercise room, media room, access to almost every form of entertainment at his fingertips—and yet he had nothing to do. Logan carried his luggage to the bedroom and unpacked. Then he wandered through the empty house, trying to find something to do. He was certain he could call Grant and a party would materialize in an hour. Logan went over to the bar and picked up a bottle, staring at it before setting it down. As much as he wanted a drink, that wasn't going to make him feel better. So he locked up and went to the bedroom, turned on the television, and cleaned up before climbing under the covers. Maybe he could just sleep and figure out what to do in the morning.

But sleep didn't come. Logan tossed and turned, wishing he could drop off, but his mind kept churning, a damned movie of every stupid thing he had done wrong playing behind his eyes. By the time he did fall asleep, out of exhaustion, he was unsettled as hell and no closer to any sort of clear path.

He woke at eight, the same time he and Brit had been getting up, pulled on a light robe, and wandered the house, hoping for some sort of answer to a question he wasn't even sure how to frame. In the past he might have called Carlton or Grant, but they weren't going to help. In fact, he wondered if they weren't part of the problem. Damn, he wished he still had his father. More than anything, he wanted to be able to pick up the phone and just call him to ask his opinion. The fact was, there was no one he could turn to, so Logan had to find his answers on his own.

Logan wasn't hungry, but he made some coffee and settled on the sofa under a light blanket, picked up that damned script for *Over the Moon*, and got reading. Maybe that was a place to start.

HOURS LATER Logan set aside the red-bound pages, blinking and swearing under his breath. Brit was right—the script and the part they wanted him to play were both incredible. He messaged to find out what the plans were for dinner and asked if Brit wanted him to pick him up. Logan had just set his phone aside when Carlton called.

"What's going on?" he asked. "I just read the script Archie sent over."

"That's really great," Carlton said softly. "Look, I'm calling because… well… I wanted to tell you that there's been an accident. Last night." His words seemed disjointed.

"What sort of accident?" Logan checked his messages and didn't see one from Brit. His chest suddenly felt like an elephant was sitting on it. "Who?" God, he had to know.

"It's Grant Little," Carlton said. "I don't know much, but he went to the clubs last night and stayed out late. One of my friends told me that they saw him on Melrose and that he was really wasted." Carlton groaned softly.

"Did he try to drive? Did he hurt someone?" God, this was terrible.

"No. But he'd had too much to drink and decided he wanted to cross Melrose in the middle of the block, in heavy traffic."

Logan managed to sit down before his legs went out from under him.

"He was hit by a driver trying to beat a light." Carlton grew quiet.

"Is he in the hospital?" Logan asked.

"No. He didn't make it that far," Carlton told him. "I'm in the car and on my way over. This is going to be hard. I thought we could sit, talk, and toast one to your old friend." Carlton sounded so reasonable. "It's probably the kind of thing Grant would have wanted. I'll be there in less than ten minutes."

Logan shook his head. That wasn't what he wanted. But after thinking for most of the night with a clear heart, things had begun to come into focus for the first time in quite a while. "Okay." He ended the call and was about to set the phone aside when Brit's response to his message came through. Immediately, Logan asked him to please come over… and to hurry.

I need you, please, he sent and then sat in the chair, afraid to move until someone arrived. God, he hoped

Brit wasn't so mad at him that he didn't come. Not that he'd blame him. Trust was a fragile thing, and Logan had blown a lot of that out of the water. Brit had told him about his dad, and Logan knew that drinking and being out of control frightened him. He had promised himself that no matter what, he wouldn't hurt Brit, and he had. Now he could only hope that Brit could forgive him enough to help, because Logan felt like he was drowning, and he needed a lifeline.

CARLTON ARRIVED, and Logan led them outside into the shade of the pool house around the sparkling water.

"I'm really sorry about Grant," Carlton said. "Give me a minute." He hurried back into the house and returned with two crystal glasses and a bottle of single malt scotch. He poured a slug into each glass and handed one to Logan. Then he sat down on one of the chaises, stretched out, and made himself comfortable. "To Grant. He was a good man and a good friend." Carlton lifted his glass, and Logan did the same. He was about to take a drink, but he paused with the glass an inch from his lips.

"Don't you see anything wrong in this?" Logan asked. "I mean, Grant died because he drank himself into a stupor and then walked into oncoming traffic." He held the glass still, looking into the amber liquid with its temptation of warmth and the enticement that it could make the loss easier. But it couldn't—and Logan *wanted* to feel the loss of his friend right now. Grant deserved that.

"He loved to party. That was one of his best traits. Everyone had a good time when Grant was around, and I think the best way to remember him is to have a party of our own... so to speak." Carlton emptied his glass and poured himself some more.

"Yes, he did. But was that all there was to him?" Logan tried to think and realized that their friendship had been nothing but a big party. Either Logan went to Grant's or Grant brought the party to Logan. They went to clubs or out to the cabaret, but it was always a good time. "Do you know about his family? What about his parents?"

Carlton shrugged, and Logan set his glass aside. "I spent time with him at some of the parties, but I didn't know him that well. He was your friend more than mine."

And yet here Carlton was, trying to get a drunk-fest going in his honor. "Grant was a whole person and more than just a party guy." Logan sat back, looking up at the blue sky peeking through the gray haze in the distance. "But did you know anything about that? I don't." And that thought was almost enough to have Logan reaching for his glass again.

What an asshole he'd been all these years. Grant was the party guy, and that was what they did. Parties, guys, fun, booze that flowed like water… it was always there. But he had never bothered to look any deeper. Yeah, Grant was his friend, but what kind of friend had he been in return? Their lives had intersected in one party that had lasted, in some way or form, for four years.

"He was Grant," Carlton said.

Logan turned just to look at him. "That's all you can say?" He swallowed hard as the breeze blew through the yard.

Carlton shrugged as Logan's phone vibrated with a message from Brit. He told him to come out by the pool, and as soon as Brit opened the doors, Carlton tensed.

"He didn't know Grant," Carlton groused as Brit came right over.

"What's going on?"

"We're toasting Grant. He died last night," Carlton said before drinking some more of the scotch. "Why don't we call a bunch of his friends and have a party as a huge sendoff?"

The idea nearly made Logan sick. "I think you've had enough." He took the bottle away and handed it to Brit. "And I think you should call a cab to take you home."

Carlton practically jumped to his feet. "Me? Why?" He tossed his arms outward and nearly threw the glass. Liquid splashed onto the grass and paving stones. "What is it with you and him?" The wildness in Carlton's eyes was a little frightening.

Logan sat up, trying to remain calm. "What is it with *you*?" Logan asked, taking Carlton's glass and setting it aside.

"Me? I only ever wanted what was best for you!" Carlton nearly screamed as Brit came to stand beside Logan. Brit didn't touch, but his support was right there nonetheless. "I did everything I could for you. I put my life on hold for you and…." He glared at Brit hard enough that Logan tensed, wondering if he was going to try to hit him. "You take up with… with…."

"That's enough," Logan snapped. "More than enough. I don't understand what's gotten into you."

"I do," Brit said gently as he threaded his fingers with Logan's. "Carlton is in love with you." He said it so casually. "Or at least he thinks he is."

"What would you know about it?" Carlton snapped, lunging forward. He brought his hand back, glaring at Brit with cold hatred.

Logan could feel Carlton racing toward Brit even before he saw it. This was no movie set, but he had been trained by enough people to be able to fight and block. Without a moment's hesitation, he lunged forward. No one was going to hurt Brit if he could help it. Logan loved him more than anything, and the notion of Brit hurting sent a raging heat through him like nothing else ever had. Logan knocked Carlton's hand away and then grabbed him by the arm and propelled him, half stumbling, across the yard.

"I think you need to cool off." He pushed Carlton into the pool, and he came up sputtering and reaching for the side. "I think that's enough."

"But—"

"No, Carlton. I think it's *more* than enough." He knelt down. "You say you wanted what was best for me, but are pills and alcohol really what was best, or was it just enough so I'd need you even more?" He wondered how he could have been so blind for so damned long. He shook his head. "You and I are done. I'll pay you through the end of the month, but I'm having all accesses changed." He backed away as Carlton climbed out of the pool, dripping everywhere, his clothes clinging to him.

"This isn't the last of this." Carlton sputtered as he flapped his arms like some demented duck to try to shake off some of the water. "Is this how you treat people who care for you?" he yelled, his usual calm façade completely blown away.

Brit patted Logan's back. "Really. That's the best you can come up with?"

"I know plenty about you—"

"And if you remember, you signed a nondisclosure document when you were hired. Archie has a copy, and so does my lawyer. Remember that. You break it, and I will make sure they hound you for as long as possible." Logan saw red as he stood straight and tall for the first time in what seemed like years. "You were what I needed at one time, but I don't think the two of us are a fit any longer." Look at him being the reasonable one and trying to defuse the situation.

"I always had your best interests at heart," Carlton challenged. "I did everything I did for you." This so-called devotion suddenly seemed to border on the obsessive, especially with the wild look in Carlton's eyes that chilled Logan to the bone. Carlton might think this was love, but it wasn't. "Okay, so the boy toy is right, I do have feelings for you. I've always loved you."

Logan could see it now. The closed-off behavior and the way Carlton ran interference. Logan had always thought that was because he was trying to protect Logan, but now he could see it for something else: a way to keep others out of Logan's life so Carlton could keep trying to get close. "But I don't feel the same way, and I never will. That isn't how I think of you." God, the pills, the booze—all of it was kept close at hand, and Carlton was always ready to offer him something to make him feel better or help him sleep. Was that all just a ploy to try to keep Logan under his influence?

"Why?" Carlton asked, still dripping on the pavement, his anger dissipating to hurt. Logan wondered just how good of an actor Carlton might be. "I was always here, and I looked after you. Why couldn't you see me?"

Logan shook his head. This conversation was becoming more surreal by the second. Brit squeezed his hand just to remind Logan that he was there. "I need someone different in my life. I know this is hard for you to understand, but I need to surround myself with different people. Like I said, I'll pay you through the end of the month per our agreement, but I need to move on, and so do you."

"This is all because of *him*," Carlton challenged, his demeanor changing again.

"No. This has nothing to do with Brit. This is about me and what I need right now." He remained calm. "Now, I suggest you go out the side gate and get an Uber or something. We're done here." God, Logan was *more* than done. Now that the scales had fallen from his eyes, he could see what Carlton had been doing: the manipulation, the way he controlled him and made him dependent. Even why he'd shown up in Mendocino. Logan had been afraid he was losing his grip, but maybe the one slipping had been Carlton instead.

Logan stood his ground, expecting some other kind of assault, but Carlton's shoulders slumped, and he turned and plodded out through the side gate, which Logan locked after him.

"I'm sorry," Brit said.

Logan shook his head. "I should have seen what he was doing long before this. But I was too busy and wrapped up in my own shit." He blinked. "What bothers me is that I let him run my life and have so much influence over me. It was like he controlled so much of what I did."

Brit nodded. "I never liked him."

Logan chuckled. "I know that. Why didn't you say something?" That was probably a stupid question.

"I hinted a few times." Brit seemed nervous, shifting his weight from foot to foot. "But it wasn't my place. We've known each other a short time, and Carlton has been your personal manager for years. No, I didn't like him, and I still don't, mainly because I saw what he was doing to you. Why do you think I kept you away from him while we were shooting? I figured that even if you were tired, good food, rest, and care were going to do you more good than that shit he kept getting you to swallow."

Brit turned and walked back to where Logan and Carlton had been sitting, and picked up Logan's glass.

"He poured it for me, but I didn't drink it," Logan said. "I couldn't. He wanted to remember Grant's death when he was drunk off his ass by getting *me* drunk. It was wrong, and I don't want to live that way. I meant what I said when I asked for help. I need it. I can't continue to live the way I have been."

Brit set the glass down on the table with a soft clink and came over to him. "I'm so damned proud of you. Did what happened to Grant really get to you?"

"It was part of it. After I came back here and spent the evening alone, I had some time to really think. There was no crap in my system, no sleeping pills or God knows what else I've been given. My head was clear, and I could really think without a load of pressure." He sat down on the chaise and tugged Brit down as well, gathering him into his arms. "I know I hurt you with what happened earlier in the week. I reacted and didn't stop to think, and I know I scared you too. Hell, I scared myself. I never imagined being that out of control." But he probably had been on many occasions. Logan had lost control of his life, and he needed to get it back. And like it or not, that wasn't Carlton's fault but his own. He had let alcohol and many other things take him over.

Logan picked up the glass on the table and took a deep look into the amber liquid with all its seductiveness, and then slowly turned the glass over, pouring it away. He wished he could say that he felt better and that everything had changed, but it hadn't. The biggest difference, though, was that he felt like he was in control.

"Don't do that again, okay?" Brit told him. "You could have missed out on a great part. And I know you love what you do."

Logan tightened his hold, pressing his cheek against Brit's. "I do." He turned lightly to kiss him. "And I love you. I know you said it earlier, and I was too angry and stuck in my own head to really react to it, but I do." He sighed and lifted his gaze toward the hazy sky. "I never would have gotten my head pulled out of my ass if it weren't for you." He watched as Brit turned, and then he kissed him.

"I already said it, but I love you too," Brit said, pulling back. "But…." His gaze flared.

"What?"

"If we end up like one of those Hollywood couples, their intimate lives splashed on the fronts of tabloids or some such shit like that, I'm going to do like you did to Carlton and throw you in that damned pool. I won't have our lives lived that way. You and I are gay. It's that simple. You're in the spotlight, which means if we're together, then I will be too."

Logan nuzzled the base of his neck. "Sweetheart, you are going to be in the spotlight in your own right soon enough. I know it."

Brit nodded. "Yeah. Maybe. And that's my point. In public, you and I are always golden. We may disagree, but that will always be private, and it will be over before we go to bed." Damn, he was sexy when he laid down the law—especially laws that Logan could get behind. "Okay? In here, our life is our own and it's just us."

Logan put both arms around Brit. "What is it you're afraid of?" he asked.

Brit tensed. "By the nature of our jobs, we will be on set and apart some of the time." His hands shook. "I can't deal with that if I'm going to come back and find you the way I did this last time. I don't think I can take that again. I know Carlton is gone...."

"He was only part of the problem. I took the damned pills and did what he said without question. That's on me." Logan knew he had to do more than just talk. "Come with me," he said quietly. He waited for Brit to get up before taking his hand and leading him inside.

Once he had the door closed, he went over to the bar and picked up a bottle in each hand and carried them to the sink. He opened them and turned them over, letting the contents go down the drain. He got another set of bottles and did the same. Vodka, tequila, whiskey, all of it flowing away. Brit reached for a couple of the bottles, but Logan stopped him with a touch.

"What?" Brit asked.

"This is something I have to do myself." He took the bottles and added them to the filling sink. Once all the opened bottles were empty and had been tossed in the recycling, he started grabbing the unopened ones from down below.

"No," Brit said. "Don't. If you're sure about this...." He hurried out to the garage and returned with a box. "Most of those are very expensive. If you're serious about this, then pack them away and we'll have your new assistant, whoever that is, sell them and you can donate the money to a substance abuse charity." Brit handed him the box, and Logan packed it all away. Then Brit carried it out and returned a few minutes later. "It's in my trunk. I'll take it to my place until you decide what to do."

"Good." Logan was doing his best to be firm. "And I thought I'd ask Margot if she's interested in a more permanent position. I think she's done a great job." He pulled open the refrigerator and reached for a soda. "What time are we expected at your mother's?" He needed to be thinking about something other than what he was drinking and the fact that he was scheduled to return to the set tomorrow. Well, they both were, so that should make things easier.

"In a few hours," Brit told him. "Come on. You look a little tired. Maybe we should go lie down." He grinned, cocking his head slightly to the side. "Of course, we don't have to *sleep* if you don't want to." Brit headed up the stairs. Logan closed the refrigerator door, set the soda on the counter, and hurried up after him.

CHAPTER 12

BRIT PULLED Logan's SUV up in front of the house he'd grown up in. The place was small, with just six rooms, but it was a Hollywood-style bungalow. The lot was a little bigger than most, but what made it extra special was the view from the hillside out to the sea. A small home with a multimillion-dollar view.

"Nice," Logan said.

"Mom and Dad bought it years ago, and Mom raked my father over the coals to be able to keep it." He turned off the engine, and they got out. Logan grabbed the flowers he'd had Brit stop to get, and they headed up the flagstone walk to the front door, which opened as soon as they got close.

"Sweetheart, Logan, I'm glad you could both come," she said, ushering them inside and closing the door. "I have nosey neighbors, and they don't need to know my business.

"These are for you, Cynthia," Logan said. Brit's mom gushed at the bouquet of white and yellow roses before leading them through to the veranda in back, where a man slightly younger than Brit's mother stood wearing pressed dress slacks, a blue polo, and a wide smile.

Brit made introductions, and Paul shook both their hands warmly and Mom offered them chairs. "Well, I of course know Logan by his films, and your mother tells me you've recently broken into the movies," Paul said. "That must be very exciting."

"It is, but it's a huge amount of work," Brit answered. "Though my parts are a lot smaller than Logan's."

"Not if you get that role," Logan told him. "Brit is reading for the lead in a new film that's being cast." He smiled. "If he gets it, the two of us will be working together once again. I'm signing on as one of the supporting roles."

"That's so fast," his mother said. "The first film hasn't even come out yet."

"People like my work and what I'm doing, so the casting directors are moving fast based on what they've seen I can do." Brit was nervous as all hell. This was so far from where he'd been just a few months ago.

"What are your next steps?" Paul asked. "Do you have a plan?" He was definitely an accountant.

Brit turned to Logan and let him answer. "I suppose the first thing I need to do is hire a new personal manager. I let mine go today."

Paul leaned forward. "Was he your business manager?"

Logan shook his head. "No. I have a professional firm that handles those things for me. He made sure I showed up to appearances on time, took care of the things at the house if I needed it, that kind of thing. Carlton also worked with my agent and I suppose the financial managers if there was anything that needed doing." Brit saw Logan start to pale.

"I'd suggest you let your managers know that he no longer works for you right away and have them audit any accounts that he might have been able to use. It wouldn't be the first time someone had their hand in the cookie jar." What Paul said made sense to Brit.

"I'll do that."

"If you don't mind my saying, send them a message now so it's done and they're notified. Who knows what he's doing right now?"

Brit snickered. "The first thing he needed to do was go home and put on dry clothes. Logan sent him for an unexpected swim in the pool." That had been a sight.

"Does he have a credit card?" Paul asked.

Logan paled, pulling out his wallet. "An Amex."

"Call them right now. Put a stop on the card, and if he made unauthorized purchases, they can be handled. The sooner the better." Paul seemed on the ball, and Logan excused himself to make some calls.

"Are things okay between you?" Mom asked.

"They seem to be. He had a shock today. A friend got drunk and tried to walk across Melrose in traffic. He didn't make it, and Logan had an epiphany and dumped out the alcohol. It's been a difficult one for him, but I think he made some decisions that will help him move to a better place."

"Son of a bitch!" Logan's voice carried into the room. "No, those are not authorized." He closed the door, and Brit bit his lower lip.

"I'm sure he's going to be okay," Mom told him.

Brit was relieved, in a way. Not that he wanted Logan to be taken advantage of, but if Carlton was trying to pull some crap, then at least he could be sure he had done the right thing. He knew Logan would feel bad about letting Carlton go. There had been more than a professional relationship between them, but in the end, business was business, and Carlton was doing more harm than good.

"I'm sorry," Logan said when he returned, taking the chair next to Brit. "As I was on the phone, Carlton was trying to pay for a large purchase down on Melrose. They denied it and canceled the card. I had them invalidate mine as well, and they're sending me a new one."

"Did he make charges before you got to it?"

Logan nodded. "I'll get the bill and turn it in to my lawyer. He's really good at scaring the crap out of people. We can also deduct what he spent from his final pay. It will come out in the end, and he isn't going to be happy."

"When you talk to the business managers, have them run a credit report and make sure there aren't any cards out there that he might have taken out in your name," Brit suggested. "They should be able to do that right away. At least you'll know for sure that he's out of your life." Brit leaned against Logan's shoulder.

"Good idea. Now let's talk about something more interesting than Carlton, like my last trip to the dentist." He grinned, and the others chuckled. Brit smiled, because the more he was around Logan, the real man, the more he loved him. "Do you play golf?" Logan asked Paul.

"God yes," Mom said. "Paul has been trying to teach me."

"Excellent. Maybe we could play sometime when I'm not filming. I have a contact at the Sherwood in Thousand Oaks. I can get us a tee time."

"You're kidding. That's one of the Jack Nicklaus–designed courses. I always wanted to play there." He seemed tickled, and Mom got up to get drinks and snacks. Brit went to help her.

"I like him, Mom," Brit told her. "He's nice, and he seems to really like you." He hugged her and was glad she was happy. Mom had spent too much time alone, and she deserved some real happiness. "Are you serious about him?"

She nodded. "I'm not going to rush into anything, but at my age, playing hard to get is off the table too. He has a home of his own, so we share time between the two, and eventually we're thinking we'll sell his house and he can move in here." Her smile made its way to her eyes, and Brit hugged her tightly.

"I'm glad you're happy."

"And things are working out for you too." She grinned at him. "Just think about it. You landed yourself a movie star."

Brit looked out to where Logan sat talking with Paul. "I got lucky."

"You know the whole alcohol-and-pills thing is going to be hard for him to walk away from," Mom said with concern in her eyes. "But he took the first step."

Brit nodded. "He asked for help, and I'm going to make sure he gets it. I'm going to ask around tomorrow, because I'm willing to bet there's an AA group of some sort at the studio itself." He couldn't look away from where Logan sat. Not that he even needed to see Logan—he drew his attention even when his eyes were closed and they were in different rooms. If he was nearby, Brit knew it.

"So what's next?" Mom asked. "Will you be sending out change-of-address forms?" Sometimes she was so cute.

"Not right away. We haven't talked about things like that yet, and I don't want to rush him. Logan has a lot going on, and we spend enough time together at the studio. I think for now we'll continue as we are. Give things some time." He swallowed.

Mom never missed much. "He hasn't asked you, has he?" Sometimes he wished she wasn't quite so observant.

"No. And that has to be his decision and something he does on his own." He narrowed his gaze. "No mentioning it to him or hinting. Please—he's important. He's everything—and I don't want to mess it up."

"He's the man you love," she supplied, and Brit nodded. "Sometimes I wonder what happened to you. As a boy, you had to have everything right now, and here you are being patient and willing to wait until he's ready." She sighed a little.

"Things change," he told her. "And he's worth waiting for." He glanced out once more. "Come on, let's get this out there before they think we've abandoned them." He picked up the cheese plate and the crackers while his mom got the hummus, and they went outside. He set the plate on the table and sat next to Logan, taking his hand. He and Paul were still talking, and Brit remained quiet, leaning slightly against Logan's shoulder, content.

For the next half hour or so they talked, and then his mom and Paul excused themselves and left him and Logan outside alone. "This is an amazing view."

"Yeah. I used to sit out here sometimes and watch over the city. It's easy to dream from up here." Brit turned to Logan. "But I never thought I'd get my heart's desire until you came along." He threaded their fingers together as the sun began to set.

"Boys, dinner will be a few minutes," his mom said from behind them. Brit didn't want to move. It was quiet, the last of the peace they'd have for a while. Tomorrow they would be back on set or on location, and everything would start up again. But for now, Brit closed his eyes and scooted closer to Logan.

"Are you ready for tomorrow?"

Brit hummed softly. "Yeah. I think we should go over our scenes when we get home. There's still a lot for us to do. Well, you more than me. But we're going to nail this, and *The Anti-Assassin* is going to be a hit."

"And if it's not?" Logan asked, tension filling him.

Brit shrugged. "Then the next one will be. You watch. This is a good film, and people are going to love it. Everyone loves an antihero. I mean, how many James Bond or Batman films have there been? This is going to join them." He turned and lightly stroked Logan's cheek. He loved the feel of him so much. "And we'll do everything we can to make it a success." Logan nodded and grew quiet. "Are you thinking about Grant?" Brit guessed.

"Yeah. That could have been me," he whispered as the light began to fade. "Hell, if it wasn't for you, I could have been with him and the two of us could have decided to make that walk together." He shivered, and Brit shifted closer. "There were so many times when I woke up and couldn't remember what had happened the night before. I was so lost, and I didn't even know it. Hell, I thought I had my shit together and that I was handling it. But I wasn't, and I hadn't been for a long time." He leaned his head against Brit's.

"I didn't mean to fall in love with you," Brit whispered. "I really didn't. I thought you were nice, but your world was so different from mine, and I couldn't figure out what you could see in me. Sometimes I still can't."

Logan touched his chin with the tips of his fingers. "What I saw was the one person on earth who looked through all my bullshit to the real me. I was a mess, and you saw something in me that no one else did. And you cared." His voice cracked. "And for the record, I didn't mean to fall in love with you either, but I couldn't fight it. You took hold of my heart, and I was a goner." He brought their lips together in a kiss that sizzled with heat and passion under a surface of deep love that made Brit wish this moment would last forever.

A familiar throat clearing had Brit smiling as he backed away. "I think it's time for dinner."

Logan nodded but didn't comment. He simply held Brit's gaze for a few seconds, as if in a silent promise that they'd pick this up when they got home. Brit agreed and only hoped his impatience didn't show as they went inside.

"DID YOU have a good break?" Chris asked when he stopped by the trailer the following morning. Both Brit and Logan had been to wardrobe and makeup and were ready for their call to set.

"We did. Thank you for everything. Your hospitality was a game changer." Brit smiled as Logan came up next to him and slid an arm around his waist.

"Damn, you look good," Chris told Logan.

"I have my head screwed on straight, and I took your advice. Carlton is gone, and I'll be speaking to Margot later today." He didn't say anything about an

AA meeting, but Brit had found one that met on studio grounds, and Logan said he intended to go during a meal break.

"Well, I don't think he's gone completely. Apparently Harris has someone new on his staff. I told Harris he isn't welcome on the set and got overruled by one of his backers." Chris shook his head. "That damned guy is like a bad penny. I thought you should both know."

"Damn, that was fast," Brit said. Logan sighed and slipped toward the back of the trailer. "Thank you for telling us."

Chris nodded, told them to be on set in thirty minutes, and then left the trailer. Brit closed the door, fuming as he went to the back, where Logan sat on the side of the bed, smiling as he talked on the phone.

"Yes, I can prove it. He didn't have permission. I have registered the charge as fraud with the credit card company, but I doubt it will go very far. I also don't want the store to suffer. But I know they have security cameras." Logan was clearly working on something. "Thank you. Let me know what you need from me." He ended the call and stood. "We should get out there." Damn, he was calm.

"Do you want to tell me what's going on?" Brit asked. "I assume this has to do with Carlton's shopping spree."

"It does, and I'm working an angle. Now let's go."

Damn, Brit liked this calmer, more capable version of Logan. He stopped him and whipped Logan around, kissing him hard. Hell, he wanted to climb the man before pushing him down on the bed and seeing how many filming sessions they could ruin with their noise.

"Calm and collected does it for you?" Logan asked.

"You better fucking believe it."

"Good to know." Logan took his hand, and they walked to the set to get ready for shooting.

THE DAYS and weeks passed in a blur of activity. Brit finished up his work on *The Anti-Assassin* and did some pick-ups for his other role. He had gone in for his screen test but hadn't heard a word from Archie or anyone. "I'm sorry," Logan told him before one of the final days of shooting. "I really thought you would have been perfect in that role."

"Did you hear who they cast?" Brit asked. If he didn't get it, he hoped he'd lost out to a big name.

"No. I only heard that they had made their choice." Logan pulled his phone out of his pocket as it continued vibrating in his hand. "Archie." He answered it, and Brit turned away to give him some privacy. "Brit, why aren't you answering your phone?"

He pulled it out of his pocket and held up the blank screen before plugging it in. It powered up and then buzzed with multiple messages. Logan tapped his shoulder and handed him his phone.

"God, I thought I was going to have to go over there and find you." Archie sounded breathless. "They made their decision. You are their Jason Russell. You got the part." He sounded even more excited. "The producers wanted a new face as the character, and you killed in your audition. They're talking about an entire franchise, and you'll be the face of it. I need an answer right away. The rest of the cast is set, and they have been looking for you for months, they just didn't know it. Principal shooting will start in two months, and they expect it to last four months, with additional call-backs and follow-up work." Brit turned to Logan and shot him a thumbs-up, grinning. "I'm still negotiating money, though it isn't going to be huge. But if this turns out, you'll be tops for the next pictures."

Brit was speechless. "I...." He couldn't seem to breathe.

"They need an answer today—"

"Oh," Brit squeaked. "Yes. I think the script is amazing, and I want the role." He grinned. "Please do your magic and let me know the next steps. I'd really like to meet some of the people I'll be working with."

"It's a great supporting cast, and the leading lady is Heather Weatherly. She's a doll to work with, and you'll come out of this as close friends, I'm sure." Archie ended the call because he needed to get the ball rolling.

"I got it," Brit told Logan. "I got the damned part. He said they've been looking for months. They wanted a fresh face, and that turned out to be me." His eyes unfocused a little, and he launched himself into Logan's arms. "My God, I can't believe this. You know, I should write a book: *From Oh My God to Jesus Christ in Three Months*." He laughed at his own joke in reference to his voice-over work.

Logan hugged him tight. "Does anyone know about that particular work? I mean, there are people who will recognize you."

"Archie does. He wasn't concerned at all. It was uncredited. But he did say that when I'm asked about what I did before I was discovered, to be honest and even play it up. Laugh it off and it will be a nonissue." He really loved his agent. Archie was brilliant in a lot of ways.

A knock sounded, and Margot poked her head in. "They're almost ready for you."

"Excellent," Logan told her. "Do you have a minute?" She came inside. "I fired Carlton, and you've been doing a great job. So Brit and I were wondering if you'd like to work for me as my personal assistant."

She smiled. "That would be great. They brought me on here as a temp, so...."

"Good. When I have a little more time, we'll talk details, and I'll get you in touch with my business manager so they can get you on board." He squeezed Brit's hand. "Thank you." She practically floated out of the trailer as he and Logan left behind her and headed to the set.

BRIT STAYED away from Carlton for the next few days. He fawned over Harris, not that Brit cared. He was just glad Carlton was out of Logan's life. He could act any way he wanted as long as he kept his distance, and Logan gave him a wide berth as well, even when Carlton kept trying to speak to him.

"I wish he'd go away," Logan said quietly between takes.

Brit nodded. "Just ignore him. We're coming to the end, after all." They had spent weeks filming on location, and this was the last of the studio shots. Then, if he understood properly, the team would shoot the last of the exteriors and the film would be in the can, as they said. Brit was ready for this one to be done. They could take a few weeks off before starting their new project.

"And Margot is working out great. She's a big help, and she knows how to stay out of the way."

"Yeah, but what about him? It pisses me off that he tried to steal from you and then threatened you when you tried to take it out of his pay." Brit hated anyone who wanted to take advantage of Logan. Just because he was successful didn't mean he should be a target.

"It will be fine," Logan told him.

"Are you two going to work or make eyes at each other?" Harris sniped, and Logan flipped him off before getting into position. Things had not improved, and Chris was losing patience with his one-act wonder. Logan had had to work extra hard to compensate for Harris's lack of skill. "Carlton, I could use a drink." He settled in his chair as Carlton headed to the catering area.

"What's that?" Brit asked, nudging Logan.

"That is the LAPD. I pressed charges and helped them gather the evidence against Carlton." Logan smiled as Harris stalked over to where Carlton was being arrested. The police kept him back.

Once the officers had read Carlton his rights and led him away, Logan approached Harris. "If I were you, I'd cancel any credit cards you gave him to use and have your people look carefully into any money he handled." Harris was stunned and simply nodded.

"He told me you fired him because of Brit," Harris mumbled. "He was stealing?"

"He tried," Logan answered and turned away before all three of them were called to the set to film one of the final scenes.

"That's a wrap," Chris announced once he had stopped rolling, and everyone clapped. Brit hugged Logan and rested his head on his chest. This was over, and Logan had done an amazing job. While others opened bottles of champagne, Brit and Logan celebrated with sparkling water.

"Are you ready to go home?" Logan asked, and Brit nodded. "Good." He smiled, and everyone around them seemed to grow spontaneously quiet. "Then maybe I should ask if you want to come home with me permanently and make your home with me."

"Awww," a few others said around them, but Brit barely heard.

"Are you sure?" he asked. Logan was just getting his life together, and Brit didn't want to put any additional pressure on him. The warmth shining back at him from Logan's eyes told him everything he needed to know.

"I am." Logan cradled his cheeks in his hands. "I love you, and I don't mind saying it in front of everyone. I want you in my life, my home, and my bed. I want you to be the last person I see at night and the first one in the morning."

"Damn, you sure know how to sweet-talk a guy," Brit said as he nodded. "Yes."

Then Logan hugged him hard before kissing his breath away to cheers and applause. Damn, it seemed that he was going to get his Hollywood ending even when the cameras weren't rolling.

EPILOGUE

THE ANTI-ASSASSIN turned out to be a hit. Logan was praised and loved even more for his performance, and a sequel was in the works and scheduled to start production in a matter of weeks. The script had been altered and Brit's character survived and had been expanded, and it was now a major supporting role. Brit was looking forward to that, because it would be the first time he and Logan had worked together since *Over the Moon*, and quite frankly, he was thrilled at the idea.

"Are you ready?" Logan asked as the car moved ahead, about to reach the front of the theater.

Brit smiled brightly. "Yes." He squeezed Logan's hand and kissed his knuckles. Then he settled back in the seat, leaning against Logan. Brit had moved in with

Logan almost a year ago, and they were happy. The hardest part was the separation, but both of them racked up airline miles to spend time together when they were on location. The work was rewarding, though the time spent apart was hard. "It's going to be a few minutes."

Logan looked amazing in his traditional tuxedo and black tie. Brit hadn't opted for anything so traditional, and while he was in a black tux, his cummerbund and tie were deep red, and the tie had been studded with crystals because he was damned well going to be different. "You look amazing," Logan whispered as he leaned closer, nuzzling the base of Brit's neck just about the time that Brit's nerves started to get the better of him.

Finally they pulled up, and Logan got out of the car. Brit followed, and Logan laced their fingers together as they walked up the red carpet past a sea of reporters and photographers, the flashes nearly blinding. Brit waved and smiled, while Logan did the same.

"How does it feel to be nominated for an Oscar for your first leading role?" one of the reporters asked. "Do you think you'll win?"

Brit paused. "You know, it really is an honor to be nominated, and I'm thrilled that my work was good enough to stand in the company of the other amazing nominees. As for how it feels, I'm over the moon." He flashed a mega smile as the reporters chuckled at his joke.

Logan answered a few questions as well, keeping their fingers laced together. It was hard to see in all the glare and lights, so Brit stayed close to Logan, who waved, answered a few more questions, and then tugged them off to the side for a quick red-carpet interview and photo opportunity.

Then they went inside, and Brit took his seat next to Logan, keeping as calm as he could until the ceremony

began. They applauded for the early awards, and then
Harris stepped onto the stage as presenter. Fortunately
he had largely returned to his television work and they
didn't cross paths often.

"The nominees for Best Supporting Actor are…."
Brit tried to be calm as the nominations were read. "Logan Steele for *Over the Moon*" came last.

Brit knew he wasn't going to win for Best Actor
despite the surprise nomination. There were too many
great performances, and he was just too new. So whatever happened with his own nomination was less important than right now. *This* was what had kept him up
at night.

Brit held Logan's hand, knowing he was tense but
trying not to let it show. Still, he could tell that Logan
was about ready to crawl out of his skin.

"And the winner is…," Harris said and opened the
envelope. Brit held his breath and Logan squeezed his
hand as time seemed to hold still. "Logan Steele for
Over the Moon."

In an instant, Brit was on his feet next to Logan. He
hugged him and then stepped back to let him head up
onto the stage. He clapped as the rest of the audience
got to their feet, the applause so intense it was nearly
deafening.

Brit barely saw Logan accept the award through
the water in his eyes, but he smiled and blinked it away,
knowing the cameras would be looking for him. Still,
he clapped and watched Logan with all the pride he
could muster as he took his place at the podium.

"There are so many people to thank, and it's too
much to list them all. The members of the Academy,
everyone associated with *Over the Moon* who worked
to make this film something truly special. But mostly

I have to thank my partner, Brighton Stevens." They had decided to use his full name rather than Brit for his acting credits. "He was the one who convinced me to take this part, and he supported me through some of the toughest times of my life. Brit saw something special in me at a time when I didn't see it in myself." Logan turned toward where Brit sat. "This award is as much for you as it is for me." He held the award in both hands, extending it toward him. "I love you forever."

Brit was in tears, and he knew the damned cameras were on him at that moment, but he didn't give a damn. The music started, and Logan said a final thank-you as he left the stage to applause.

Brit knew he could go backstage to find Logan, but his legs didn't want to work. A man sat next to him to fill Logan's seat until Logan came out and replaced him. "You were amazing," Brit said, taking Logan's hand. "Thank you."

Logan smiled and shook his head. "I love you." While the next presenter was on stage, Logan reached into his pocket. Brit's eyes widened as he withdrew a ring box and pulled it open. A gold man's ring set with a single sapphire caught the light. "Will you…?" Logan asked.

As if by magic, the thousands of people around them disappeared and only the two of them remained. "Yes," Brit whispered, and Logan slipped the ring onto his finger. In that moment, surrounded by Hollywood glitterati and everyone who was anyone in town, for a few seconds, they were the brightest stars in the sky.

Keep reading for an excerpt from
Don't Let Go by
Andrew Grey.

CHAPTER 1

ROBERT CLOSED the door to his dressing room and sat on the sofa, shutting his eyes so he could have a few moments of peace. Not that he was likely to get that. There were too many damn people who wanted a piece of him, and they weren't about to let something as inconsequential as a door stop them.

Performing usually sent him through the ceiling—the excitement of the crowd, being onstage doing what he'd always loved, what he'd dreamed about since his dad have given him his first guitar at seven years old. He still had that guitar. Didn't play it anymore, but he still had it. He was starting to feel a little like that instrument: old, tired, and maybe a little bit of a relic. Not that his career would reflect that. He was at the top of his game, in terms of audiences and the number of times his songs were downloaded. If that was the real measure of success in this industry, then he was certainly a megasuperstar. Not that he felt like it.

His real name was Robert Cummings, but his manager and the record label that had first signed him had thought that name was too plain and didn't say "music star," so onstage he was Avery Rivers. Over the years, that name had enveloped more and more of his life. From his start in the recording studios and onstage, it had taken over television, online, radio—you name it. Avery Rivers had become so big that plain old Robert barely existed at all anymore.

Like he knew it would, the door swung open. Robert didn't bother to look up.

"That was something else," his manager, Glenn Hopper, said, tugging off his cowboy hat to fan himself with it. "You were on fire, my friend." He didn't bother closing the door, which meant he was expecting more people.

Ray followed behind, hooking the door closed with one of his boots.

"We have a meeting tomorrow morning at eight. The record label and the tour promoter want to talk over what's next," Glenn said.

Robert ignored him. "What do you need, Ray?" he asked softly.

"Excuse me? I can't hear you." Ray stepped closer.

Robert didn't raise his voice at all. "I said, what do you want?"

Ray turned to Glenn, confused. Ray was the representative of the company that had put together the tour that had just wrapped up. Tonight had been the final stop, and Robert was tired beyond belief.

"Can Glenn and I talk, please?"

Ray shot Robert a dirty look and scowled at Glenn, but he left the room. As the door opened, a wall of sound came in, then cut off when it closed again.

Robert sighed. "God, I hate that man," he said. "Not that he's done anything wrong. It's just that he doesn't have a right to be part of every goddamned conversation I have. Sometimes I swore he was going to show up in my bathroom." He also gave Robert the creeps, but he'd never been able to put his finger on exactly why. Maybe Robert was just getting tired and less patient.

Glenn snickered. "He's not a bad guy. Just a little nervous. This was the first tour he'd been put in charge of, and he wanted to make a good impression on his bosses. We all have that kind of shit to deal with sometimes."

"Has Barry been on your ass again?" Robert asked, and Glenn shrugged.

"He is who he is. Barry makes stars in this business. That's what he knows how to do. The rest of it is completely foreign, which is why he has us to handle all the people-skills end of things." Glenn pulled over a chair, sat, and pulled out his iPad. "Anyway, I wanted to go over things for tomorrow, and then we'll get you back to the hotel." He tapped a few times. "Okay. As I was saying, there is a meeting at eight with the tour promoters, as well as the record label. Barry will be there too."

"Not eight," Robert said. "That's too damn early."

Glenn's tapping on the screen stopped and his head came up. "That's the time of the meeting, and…."

"Reschedule it to ten, please," Robert said firmly. "It's nearly midnight now, and it's going to take some time before I can get to sleep. So make it ten." He raised his gaze. "Tell Barry to reschedule the meeting at ten per my request. Because otherwise I'm not going to be there."

"You know they'll have the meeting without—" Glenn stopped when Robert held up his hand.

"No, they won't. They'll reschedule it." Robert smirked.

Glenn started typing again, and sure enough, he nodded. "All right. We'll meet at ten." He set down the tablet. "Believe it or not, that's the only thing I have for you tomorrow. The interviews and television spots have been taped." He patted Robert's shoulder. It ached something fierce, and Robert flinched slightly. Glenn didn't seem to notice. "You did an amazing job through all of this. It's been a whirlwind four months, and you were there and on point the entire time."

"Thanks, Glenn." Robert sighed and sat back on the sofa, closing his eyes again. "I want to get something to eat, something thick and juicy, and then I'm going to go to bed. So let's go." He stood and got ready to leave the room.

"How about we get you to the hotel and I'll order you up some room service? You can relax and take it easy while you eat, and there isn't going to be a crush of people asking for your autograph." Glenn opened the door, and Robert stepped out of the dressing room.

"Avery, when do you expect to release your next album?" a reporter asked. She didn't identify herself but had just the right earnest, yet smug, tinged-with-desperation look about her that was a dead giveaway.

"Soon," Robert answered without stopping.

"Is it true that you haven't actually written a single song for it and the label is getting worried?" she pressed as they continued down the hall. Those things were true, but Robert didn't acknowledge them. It wasn't his fault that he hadn't had two minutes of peace in four damned months.

They reached the stage door, and Robert passed through as security joined them, freezing out the reporter. A group of men and women waited there, all screaming as he emerged, thrusting pieces of paper at him.

Just like that, Avery burst through and he was on, the same way he'd been on during the performance. Every ounce of fatigue vanished as he smiled and took the papers to sign the name that wasn't really his.

"Hey, darlin'," he said to a girl standing next to a man who had to be her father. She was probably ten or eleven, with big blue eyes and pretty blonde hair. "What's your name?"

"Lisa," she said. She wasn't jumping and screaming like the others, but the excitement in her eyes spoke volumes. Her father put his arms around her protectively, and when the others made a little space, Robert saw the braces on her legs.

"Well, Lisa...." He flashed her a smile as she handed him a souvenir program that they'd sold out front.

"Will you sign it?" she asked.

Robert nodded. He took the book, opened it, and found a page with one of his pictures. He turned to Glenn, who handed him a black Sharpie, and signed the picture to her. Robert then remembered he was still wearing a tour cowboy hat. One of the companies had sent a hundred black hats with white bands. Robert wore them at performances and threw them into the crowd, which sent everyone into a frenzy. He took it off, signed the white band, and handed her the hat.

She held it as though it were the Holy Grail. "Thank you."

"You're welcome, darlin'."

For a few seconds, the crowd around him had dissipated, but it came roaring back as soon as he finished with Lisa. Robert signed a few more autographs as his security helped him get closer to the waiting car. The door was open, and he ducked inside. When the car door closed, he could be Robert again, slumping back on the seat. He turned, peering out the tinted windows at the already dispersing crowd. Robert watched as Lisa and her dad became visible. She waved, and Robert lowered the window to wave back at her as Glenn got in from the other side. He raised the window as the car pulled away.

"Take us to the hotel. We'll use the back entrance," Glenn told the driver, giving her all the details.

"Of course," she answered quietly, and Robert finally relaxed once again. Dinner, sleep, and then that damned meeting, and he was done and could go home.

"GOOD, WE'RE all here," Barry Stroheim said from his seat as Robert walked in.

Robert strode past the single empty seat halfway down the table and stopped at the head of the table where some guy he didn't know sat, leaning back in the chair like a bored toddler. He tapped him on the shoulder, and the man turned to look at him.

"Yeah?" the guy asked.

"Avery, this is my nephew, Lindon," Barry said.

"Nice to meet you, Lindon. Now get your ass out of my seat." Robert pointed to the other chair, and Lindon slowly stood, his perfect dark blue suit falling into place on his tall frame. Nepotism was never a good idea as far as Robert was concerned. He took the now-empty chair and smiled as Barry glared at his nephew. Glenn sat next to him, and Robert nodded to Barry, folding his hands together. "Can we get started?" he asked quietly.

"Of course," Barry said, and turned to Ray.

"The tour has been a huge success. There have been sellout crowds in every city for every concert. In some places we made adjustments to the ticket prices for the first eight to ten rows, nearly doubling them for later dates, and they sold out completely." Ray grinned, and the others looked pleased.

"You price-gouged the fans?" Robert said, scowling at him.

"These tours are expensive, and we need to recoup all of the costs. Which we've done…," Ray explained.

"And the tour has driven CD sales and downloads through the roof, even on older material," one of the label guys said. They seemed to change all the damn time, and Robert was barely able to keep up with who they were. "Avery Rivers is the hottest thing with a guitar." They all sat back smugly as though that was their doing.

"Yes, and we'd like to keep that going," Ray said. "So the tour organizers and sponsors want to exercise the option in the contract for six additional stops, with two concerts in each location." He passed out papers, and Robert took one that explained the proposed tour additions. "We'll use the next two weeks to get the word out and sell tickets, which we're sure will burn up the internet. The venues are thrilled to have us and will go into publicity mode just as soon as we give the okay."

Barry looked things over and then turned to Glenn. They both nodded as though the decision was theirs and Robert wasn't even in the room.

"Robert can rest up over the next two weeks, and then he'll be ready to go," Barry said.

At least Glenn had the courtesy to look worried, but he nodded as well. They weren't the ones who were too damn worn out to think straight half the time. Robert held his breath, his hands shaking, as they all talked around him.

"Then we're all on board, and I'll get the wheels in motion." Ray sat back as one of the record label guys cleared his throat.

"We need some—"

Robert had had enough. He smacked his hand on the table, the sound filling the room. Everyone except him jumped and all talking ceased. "That's better. Now…." Robert turned to Ray. "The tour contract states that additional dates can be added by mutual agreement."

"Yes," Ray said. "We want to exercise the option, and your people have agreed."

Robert switched his gaze to Glenn. "I'm tired and running on empty. I haven't been able to write anything new in months. My throat hurts and my head aches. I'm living on Red Bull and whatever I can get to eat after the concerts."

Glenn turned to him. "You'll have two weeks to rest." Then he looked away.

"Look here, you self-absorbed pain in the ass," Robert said without raising his voice. He needed to get everyone's attention, and more importantly, he needed to get his manager's head back where it belonged. "I know you don't know this, but I read my contracts too. The concert schedule can only be extended by mutual consent, and I will not agree." He turned to Ray. "You've done a great job managing this entire process, but I'm worn out. So last night was the end of this tour. It's time."

"But, Avery, it will—"

"I mean it. I'm done and can't take any more." Robert turned to Barry. "You're my agent, and it's your job to watch out for me. Our contract is up in six months, and if you wish to remain my agent, some things are going to have to change or I'll find new representation." Robert leaned across the table. "And I'll order a full audit of every penny for the last seven years." That was also within his rights. Not that Barry had ever given him any reason to suspect he was anything but aboveboard with the finances, but it represented a huge pain in the ass that Robert could use as a club to get his way. "I want to write and take some time for myself."

"You can do that after these additional dates. You're the hottest ticket out there right now. We need to keep that moving." Ray seemed as sincere as he could get. Suddenly Robert knew why he'd never trusted him—that arrogance.

"We will by letting me return to my music," Robert said. "Thank you, Ray, for everything. But there will be no additional dates. I need some time. Maybe in a few months we can go back out on the road, but I just can't do that right now." He scanned the expressions of every man in the room. "Just so I'm being clear, this isn't negotiable." He turned to Barry. "I mean it. You all talk around and over me as though I don't exist, but it's because of me that all of you have jobs. So I'm putting my foot down and will be making some decisions about my future." Robert was pretty proud of himself that he never raised his voice.

"You're going to write new material?" the record exec asked, seeming pleased. "That's good news. We'd like to get you recording again soon. So that sounds like a good decision to us."

"Good. Then that's what we're going to do." Robert stood. "This meeting is over. If any of you have any questions, you can forward them to Barry or Glenn. Otherwise, we're done here." He waited while Ray, Lindon, and the other executives stood, clearly wondering if they could speak with Barry. They didn't like being told no, and Robert was pretty sure they were already trying to figure out angles they could use to get what they wanted. Robert motioned for Glenn and Barry to sit where they were, and eventually everyone else left.

The door closed on the last person, and Robert sighed, leaning back in his chair.

"They aren't going to be happy," Barry said.

"So what? They don't give a damn about making me happy. The tour company is a bunch of penny-pinching vultures who don't deserve to be made happy." Robert glared at both of them. "I want you both to get that through your heads. You work for me and no one else. And…." He stared at Barry. "I. Do. Not. Work. For. You! Please remember that. I call the shots, so you do what *I* want you to. Otherwise I'll find different representation." He pushed back from the chair and stood. "Harvey with the record label is happy, and he's the only one we need to worry about."

"Not true. What about the next time we need to tour?" Barry asked.

"They'll be there with their damned hand out and you know it. Besides, they needed to be knocked down a peg or two. They treat their people like crap, and I had to step in more than once." Robert yawned and stretched. "I'm going back to the hotel to pack."

"Do you want me to make travel arrangements for you to go home?"

"To Nashville?" Robert rolled his eyes, then shook his head. He hated the house there. "I'll make my own decisions for a while. What I want you to do is figure out how I can have some time to write and produce new songs. That's what you need to worry about." He stood and wandered over to the windows of the rented conference area, peering down into Grant Park and

Buckingham Fountain. "It's what we all need to worry about, because I haven't written a note in six months. The music in my head has been silent for so long, I don't know if it will ever start again."

Robert clasped his hands behind his back, staring. He needed to find himself once again, and that wasn't going to happen in the back of a tour bus, on an airplane, or in a hotel room. Robert's music had always been a well that had bubbled up from inside. It had started when he was seven. That guitar from his dad had started the flow. Robert had learned to play in a matter of weeks and was playing the songs that were in his head by the time he was ten years old. Thankfully, Dad had sent him to music class, and he'd learned how to write his songs down, and from there the well had gushed up toward the light. Now it was dry, and he felt as brittle and parched as desert sand.

"Okay," Glenn said as Lindon returned and closed the door.

Robert closed his mouth and shook his head. He turned to Barry, saying nothing until Barry motioned for Lindon to leave again. "I know he's your nephew, but he is to have nothing at all to do with my business. I hired you, not your family."

Barry groaned. "My sister's kid, and you know how it is."

"Put him to work in the mail room or something. He isn't to have access to any of my business. Not contracts... nothing. I pay for your time and attention... not your nephew's." Robert was really feeling pissy and he hated it. "I'm sure he's a nice enough man, but he hasn't proven himself... the way you and Glenn have." He turned back to the view and tried to calm himself down and get his head back where he needed it. "Remember those first venues you booked for me six years ago?"

Barry chuckled. "The VFW halls and small-town theaters."

"Those were amazing times. Everything was new, and I threw myself into every performance, trying out new material and…." Robert's blood had pumped then, and everything had been ahead of him. "I had one cowboy hat, a single pair of good jeans, and the boots I picked up at a secondhand store. That's what I played in every night. I wore those jeans and boots until they fell apart." They'd been like old friends. The hat had been replaced years earlier after it was lost in travel. He missed all of it. "That's why I work with you. Because you were with me then, and somehow I need to feel like that again." He shook his head. It was the best way he could explain how he felt.

Barry put up his hands. "All right. I can understand that. What are you going to do?" He stood next to Robert, bumping his shoulder. "We've been through too damned much already, and I don't want to see you burned the hell out."

God, it felt good to know that Barry and Glenn, who now were both standing beside him, had his back.

"I don't know where I'm going. But, Glenn, I need for you to see that the stuff I don't take gets home and make sure everything is okay there." Glenn already had his pad out and was making notes. "Then call a Realtor and have the house put on the market." Robert expected a fight from both of them, but to his surprise, Barry patted his shoulder.

"I'm sorry I talked you into buying that place," he whispered. "I thought you'd like it."

"It was never me." Robert turned and headed toward the door, then pulled it open. "I'll be in touch."

"Where are you going to go?" Barry asked again.

"I don't know. I think I'm going to hit the road on my own for a while." Robert grinned at the horrified looks on their faces. "Don't worry. I'll still have my phone. But I need to know that both of you are there for me."

They nodded, and Robert left, heading to the elevator and down to the parking garage, where the limousine waited. He got in and told the driver to go to the nearest Ford dealership.

"Sir?" she asked.

"I wanna buy a truck."

THE FOLLOWING day, Robert was out on his own. He had a used truck loaded with the things that were important to him: some clothes, a guitar, his hat, and his boots. Everything else was on its way back to Nashville, because he didn't need it now, and he knew Glenn would take care of all of it. He headed west out of Chicago and kept going, driving all day, racing toward the sun. When it got dark, he pulled on a baseball cap and checked into a highway wayside hotel. The woman behind the desk looked at him again and again as he checked in, and Robert hurriedly grabbed his key when she offered it to him and headed to his room.

He should have thought more carefully about the possibility of being recognized.

In the hotel room, he pulled his kit out of his suitcase. Not finding what he needed, he went and got a disposable razor and trial-size shaving cream out of the vending machine, then shaved off his signature black scruff. Next, he used his beard trimmer on the longest setting to cut away his neck-length black curls. It was difficult for Robert to recognize himself in the mirror, so he doubted anyone else would know who he was. Robert cleaned up the mess into a plastic bag, tied it off, and shoved all of it in the trash. Then he left and went to get dinner.

In a small sports bar a half mile down the road, he took a seat, and the server brought him a menu. It must have been a slow sports night, because half the televisions were tuned to CMT.

"Ruthie, can we change the channel?" the man in the next booth asked as one of Robert's music videos began to play. Robert held his breath as Avery Rivers sang and played on half a dozen screens.

"No. I love this one," she said, swaying to the music. "He can eat crackers in my bed any time he wants." She turned away to take Robert's drink order, still paying half attention to the television. Robert asked for a diet soda, watching her watch him. It was surreal, and the perfect test that his change in appearance was sufficient.

"Come on, Ruthie…," the guy said, and she smacked his shoulder.

"You're just jealous because you don't look like that, and you certainly don't sound like him. Let me tell you," she sighed, "that man is God's gift to women."

Robert picked up his menu, staring at it intently. If she only knew how wrong she was about her last statement. He loved women and treated each one who worked with him with respect and didn't allow anything else from anyone. But he had never been interested, romantically, in them.

Once the video ended, she took his order for some hot wings and hurried away without giving Robert a second glance.

If he were honest, he was a little disappointed. There was something heady about being famous and having the rest of the world screaming for him and wanting to catch a glimpse of him. When he'd first started out, Robert had soaked in the attention and adulation like a sponge. That had led to some problems. Thankfully Barry had been there to provide advice and to stop him from going down the path of destruction that happened to so many.

"Where are you from?" the man at the next table asked as Ruthie brought his plate of food.

"Nashville," Robert said, then added quickly, "And Chicago before that." He needed a way to easily explain his accent. "Just passing through on my way west." He started eating, watching the television as the station broke into some news.

"With his tour over, Avery Rivers seems to have disappeared. A source has said that he declined to add six additional stops to his record-breaking tour."

Robert's appetite suddenly flew out the window.

"According to our source, Avery is worn out and wanted some time to rest and compose." The woman smiled into the camera. "Not that we can blame him. Personally, I'm waiting on pins and needles for his next album. If he has decided to take some time for himself, we wish him well, wherever he is." The program went on to the next story, and Robert pulled out his phone to send a quick text to Barry.

He got an immediate response. *I'm already on it. I'll roast that weasel Ray over a spit for this.*

Good, Robert sent. *Find out if he did it, and if so, just take care of it.* He put his phone back in his pocket and finished his dinner.

"You headed anywhere particular?" the man asked, cutting through Robert's thoughts.

"Not especially. I thought I'd take some time, go out west, see the sights, and maybe have some fun for a while before returning to work." Robert sat back, his plate empty, and drank some of his soda to relieve the burn in his mouth from the sauce. Dang, that was good.

"Colorado," the man said. "Beautiful place. Either that or head on up to Wyoming. Yellowstone is stunning, and there's nothing like those wild spaces to make a man feel alive again." He raised his beer glass, and Robert lifted his soda, finished the last of it, and left Ruthie a large cash tip when she brought the check.

"Thank you. I'll keep that in mind." He smiled and left, heading back to the hotel.

Robert spent the evening doing little, just lying on the bed and resting. Downtime was so foreign that he actually felt guilty for doing nothing.

He went to bed early and slept soundly before getting up and on the road once again. He spent most of the day crossing Nebraska. God, was it flat and uninteresting. He drove as fast and as much as he could, waiting until mountains appeared on the horizon. He veered slightly north, figuring he'd try Wyoming first, and made it as far as Cheyenne before calling it a day.

Dusty and tired from the road, Robert pulled up in front of the Plains Hotel. He parked and went inside, carrying his bag up to the front desk, marveling at the geometric coffered stained-glass ceiling.

"Do you have a reservation?" the man behind the desk asked.

"No," Robert answered, and the man pulled an "I'm sorry" face like he was going to say they were full. Avery Rivers would have been welcomed and fawned over, but Robert was just another guy.

"Let me see what we have." He typed and worried his lower lip. "How long would you like to stay? It's rather busy this weekend because of the rodeo." He sighed as he looked. "I have only two rooms available. They are both king suites with a separate parlor." He bit his lower lip once again.

Robert handed over one of his personal credit cards. "Book me in for the rest of the weekend, leaving on Monday morning."

THE BAR was hopping, and Robert squeezed his way in to get a drink, then snagged a stool, turning away from the bar to take in the scenery, and man, there was plenty of it. Men in Wranglers, huge belt buckles catching the light every now and then, Stetsons in every color, and boots in every type of skin available. The sight was gorgeous, and damn it all if his own music didn't fill the place. Someone was certainly a fan, because one song after another played, the dance floor to the side packed with people having a great time.

"You here for the rodeo?" a man next to him asked, trying to get the bartender's attention.

"Here to watch," Robert answered as his eyes darted over the compact, cool drink of water with eyes the color of the sky on a cloudless day. Fuck, he was one gorgeous guy. "It looks like it's going to be one great weekend. You got tickets too?" They were apparently hard to come by at this point. Robert hadn't minded paying, even if he had only a moderately good seat.

Still, he was here for some fun and relaxation, and to immerse himself in the country life once again.

"Oh yeah. This is a great event." The man finally got the bartender's attention and placed his order. "You here alone?" he asked, turning once again to Robert, his eyes sparkling, causing heat to build at the base of Robert's spine. It had been a damn long time since he'd allowed himself any type of carnal pleasures, and hell if his dick didn't stand up to remind him just how long it had been and that this was a man who pushed all his buttons.

"Yeah." Robert saw some of his desire reflected in the other man's eyes, and it sent his heart racing a little faster, the pit of his belly zinging and fluttering slightly. "I just got into town a few hours ago and needed something to eat." He also wanted to drink and relax. Robert had no illusions that Cheyenne was going to have any rainbow-type nightlife, but it looked like some might have found him. That was, if he could still read the signs.

Robert got a refill and slipped off his barstool to wander toward the back of the bar, where a bunch of people were watching the dance floor. The cowboy came right along with him, which in Robert's mind was a sure sign of interest. He leaned against the wall as couples line-danced their way across the floor.

"I love his music," the cowboy said from next to him.

"Me too," Robert said about his own song. He had loved it when he wrote it and recorded it, but now he'd heard it and sung it so many times…. He needed something new to get the creative juices flowing. "I'm Robert." He held out his hand.

"Zeke," the cowboy answered, shaking firmly, his touch lingering just a little longer than normal, which only upped the flutter of excitement. "I never got to see him when he was in Denver. Me and some friends talked about getting tickets, but they were sold out in minutes." Zeke sipped his beer as the song came to an end, and Robert did the same, trying not to be too obvious about watching him. "I wonder if his voice really sounds like that or if it's Auto-Tuned or something."

Robert pulled a face as his temper threatened to rise. He had never used Auto-Tune or any of that synthesized shit in his music. That was cheating as far as he was concerned. What was heard on all his recordings was truly him and nothing else. "I suspect it's real. It sounds it."

Zeke nodded. "True. How can anyone conjure up those soulful rich undertones that get you just right?"

Robert shrugged. He certainly didn't want to get too deep into a discussion of himself. It seemed wrong and was way too close to home.

Half the place was dancing, and a pretty girl in boots and a Western denim skirt came up to him, all smiles and huge eyes. "Do you dance?" she asked Robert, fluttering her eyes at him.

Robert smiled and nodded. Then he held the lady's hand and led her onto the floor. It took him two seconds before he was into the moves, and he danced to her delight, adding a little extra spring to his step.

The song ended and Robert was about to head off the floor when another lady, this one a little older, approached. She smiled and took a turn, with Zeke dancing just one person over. Robert loved line dancing. It was fun, active, and exciting, while at the same time allowed him to basically dance with the person he wanted to, in plain sight, even if it wasn't particularly socially acceptable.

"You're a fine dancer," the woman said once they'd danced their number.

"So are you." Robert excused himself to sit the next one out—or stand, as the case may be.

Zeke came over shortly after Robert took his place to watch. "Not up for more?" Zeke asked.

Robert smiled. "I'm up for quite a bit. I like to dance, but it's been a long day."

"Were you able to find a place to stay? With the rodeo in town, it can be difficult. Most of the hotels are full and have been for some time," Zeke said.

"I think I got lucky. I'm at the Plains. They had a few rooms available, and I was able to get one of the last ones. Maybe they had a last-minute cancellation or something." Robert wasn't going to admit he'd gotten one of the most expensive rooms in the hotel.

"Fancy," Zeke said softly. "I'm staying with some friends." He lowered his gaze and then slowly raised it. Robert felt it like a heated touch. "Would you like another drink?"

Robert turned to the bar, which was at least four people deep, and Zeke did the same. "There's a bar near the hotel that seems quieter," Robert offered nervously. It had been a long time since he'd played this particular game, and Robert knew he probably wasn't very good at it.

"I think that would be a good idea." Zeke's gaze traveled across the dance floor, and Robert saw a group of ladies talking together and glancing over at them.

Robert turned to leave the ever-more-crowded bar and was relieved to be outside. He inhaled the fresh, dry air deeply and waited for Zeke. He didn't want to seem like he was desperate, standing there, but only a minute later, Zeke stepped out into the night. They walked toward Robert's hotel quietly until Zeke cleared his throat.

"Have you been to Cheyenne before?" Zeke asked.

"Yes, once, some time ago." Robert smiled as they crossed the street, the marquee for one of the smaller venues he'd played years ago just down the block. Sometimes that seemed like another lifetime. "I like it here. This is a very nice, small city." He glanced at Zeke as they walked past the bar he'd intended to stop at, heading to the hotel. Robert's nerves built until they were inside and in the elevator. His doubts drifted away when they reached his floor, and as Robert unlocked the door, he wondered if this was actually going to happen.

They stepped inside, and Robert closed the door. As soon as it latched, Zeke cupped Robert's cheeks in his work-roughened hands, kissing him with all the intensity of a hurricane, and still Robert wanted more.

ANDREW GREY is the author of more than one hundred works of Contemporary Gay Romantic fiction. After twenty-seven years in corporate America, he has now settled down in Central Pennsylvania with his husband of more than twenty-five years, Dominic, and his laptop. An interesting ménage. Andrew grew up in western Michigan with a father who loved to tell stories and a mother who loved to read them. Since then he has lived throughout the country and traveled throughout the world. He is a recipient of the RWA Centennial Award, has a master's degree from the University of Wisconsin–Milwaukee, and now writes full-time. Andrew's hobbies include collecting antiques, gardening, and leaving his dirty dishes anywhere but in the sink (particularly when writing). He considers himself blessed with an accepting family, fantastic friends, and the world's most supportive and loving partner. Andrew currently lives in beautiful, historic Carlisle, Pennsylvania.

Email: andrewgrey@comcast.net
Website: www.andrewgreybooks.com

Follow me on BookBub

Everybody needs to be rescued sometime.

Veterinarian Mitchell Brannigan gets off to a rocky start with his new neighbor when someone calls the town to complain about the noise. Mitchell runs a shelter for rescue dogs, and dogs bark. But when he goes to make peace, he meets Beau Pfister and his fussy baby daughter, Jessica… and starts to fall in love.

Beau moved out to the country to get away from his abusive ex-husband, but raising an infant alone, with no support network, is lonely and exhausting. The last thing he expects is a helping hand from the neighbor whose dogs he complained about.

Mitchell understands what it's like to live in fear of your ex, and he's determined to help Beau move on. But when an unseen menace threatens the shelter and Beau, it becomes apparent that he hasn't dealt with his own demons.

With each other and a protective Chihuahua for support, Mitchell, Beau, and Jessica could make a perfect family. Mitchell won't let anything happen to them.

But who's going to rescue him?

www.dreamspinnerpress.com

ANDREW GREY

Rescue Us

MUST LOVE DOGS

Everyone needs to be rescued sometimes.

As a vet tech, Daniel is usually first in line to come to animals' aid. When he and his boss get a call about an animal hoarding situation, they expect the handful of badly treated dogs… but the tiger comes as a surprise.

Wes recently left his job to care for his sick mother. Now that she's on the mend, he needs work, and he finds it at a bustling shelter. But the animals aren't the only ones in need. His kind, chatty coworker Daniel is dealing with an abusive boyfriend—something Wes, whose father was an alcoholic, has experience handling. Wes steps up to help Daniel kick his boyfriend to the curb, but in the process, he finds himself falling for Daniel himself.

Navigating a new relationship when they both have traumatic pasts is one thing. But when a shady group starts targeting the tiger they are trying to find a zoo placement for, the stakes are raised even higher. Can Wes and Daniel come together to rescue the animals—and each other?

www.dreamspinnerpress.com

ANDREW GREY

PAINT
BY
NUMBER

Can the Northern Lights and a second-chance romance return inspiration to a struggling artist?

When New York painter Devon Starr gives up his vices, his muses depart along with them. Devon needs a change, but when his father's stroke brings him home to Alaska, the small town where he grew up isn't what he remembers.

Enrique Salazar remembers Devon well, and he makes it his personal mission to open Devon's eyes to the rugged beauty and possibilities all around them. The two men grow closer, and just as Devon begins to see what's always been there for him, they're called to stand against a mining company that threatens the very pristine nature that's helping them fall in love. The fight only strengthens their bond, but as the desire to pick up a paintbrush returns, Devon also feels the pull of the city.

A man trapped between two worlds, Devon can only follow where his heart leads him.

www.dreamspinnerpress.com

A NEW LEAF 🍂 ROMANCE

NEW LEAF

ANDREW GREY

When Dex Grippon's mother dies, he takes it as a sign—it's time to give up acting and return to his hometown. If he can find a way to save his mother's bookstore, he can preserve the one link he still has to his parents. But keeping an independent bookstore afloat turns out to be more difficult than he anticipated, and Dex isn't the only one who wonders what else his mom might have been selling.

Former cop Les Gable might be off the job, but he has to know what was going on at the bookstore, and he'll do anything to satisfy his curiosity—including befriend the new owner with an offer to help sort out his new business. Something about the bookstore doesn't smell right, and Les is going to find out what.

The problem is that his curiosity about Dex soon far outstrips his interest in what happened at the store. But as curiosity matures into love, the store's past threatens their future. Can Les and Dex untangle the mystery of the bookshop and escape with their relationship—and their lives—intact, or will the whole thing go up in smoke?

www.dreamspinnerpress.com

A NEW LEAF ROMANCE

IN THE WEEDS

ANDREW GREY

Florist to the stars Vin Robins is in high demand in LA, but he hates working for someone else. When he returns to his Pennsylvania home to help his widowed father, he finds an opportunity he never expected with his first love, but learns that someone's been taking advantage of the unused family greenhouse.

Casey Lombard wasted too much of his life denying who he is and what he wants, but he won't do that any longer. His biggest regret is letting Vin go, so running into Vin again when he gets called to investigate who planted pot on Vin's family's property sends him reeling.

Vin ignites feelings Casey thought long dead. But Casey has a daughter, and Vin is only home for a visit. Surely the bright lights of Hollywood will call him back to the City of Angels, so how can Vin and Casey build the life they both wish they had?

www.dreamspinnerpress.com